Teaching Across History

Valeaira Luppens • Greg Foreman

Alfred

© 2013 Alfred Music
16320 Roscoe Blvd., Suite 100
P.O. Box 10003
Van Nuys, CA 91410-0003

All Rights Reserved. Printed in USA.

ISBN-10: 0-7390-9261-8
ISBN-13: 978-0-7390-9261-3

TABLE OF CONTENTS

Preface 3

Great-Great-Great Inventions! 4
    Baroque Period Inventions 5
    Classical Period Inventions 5
    Romantic Period Inventions 6
    Modern Period Inventions 7

Holiday Fun 10
    Holidays—Fun! Fun! Fun! 11

The Pledge of Allegiance 16

String Story 21

Forward March 24

Compacting Composers 29

Crack the Code 35

Sail! Sail! Sail Your Boat! 41

Peer Gynt Isn't Very Sweet! 46

Thanksgiving Trivia 49
    "Over the River and Through the Woods" 52

Hansel and Gretel 56

Opera History 58

The Nutcracker 60
    Piotr Ilyich Tchaikovsky 61

Martin Luther King, Jr. 64
    Who Am I? 65
    Martin Luther King Jr. 66

Chit Chat 70

Favorite Songs 73
    What Makes a Song Great? 74

George Washington 76
    George Washington's Biography 77
    Georgie's Rap 78

A Lincoln Portrait 79
    A Lincoln Portrait, (excerpt) by Aaron Copland 80

Election Day 81

Let My People Go! 84

Bach's Court Trial 86
    Background Notes for Court Case 88
    Courtroom Procedure 89

Bumblebee Blast! 91

Nursery Rhymes 94
    Old MacDonald Had a Farm 95
    Lucy Locket 96
    Mary Had a Little Lamb 97
    Twinkle, Twinkle, Little Star 98
    Nursery Rhyme Medley 99

The Voice of the Pioneers 105
    The Voice of the Pioneers Clues 106

All That Jazz! 110

His Truth Is Marching On 114
    Julia Ward Howe 115
    Clara Schumann 116
    Women's Rights 117

The Treble Talk Show! 118

Give My Regards to Broadway! 123

Time Machine 126
    The International Society of Time Travelers 129

CD Contents (Suggested Uses) 135

Music History Internet Resources 136

About the Authors 137

Preface

Teaching Music Across History is a resource for the elementary and middle school general music teacher, as well as classroom teachers. This book will motivate students to become more actively involved in the arts by incorporating data taught in their history classroom with music. An additional benefit for the students is they will retain the information better when it is connected to the emotional hook of music. Students need a general understanding of how music and the arts are often a reflection of our culture. They also need to be aware of how historical events have shaped our civilization and customs. *Teaching Music Across History* will help your students meet item 9 of the National Standards for Music Education* ("Understanding music in relation to history and culture"), incorporate a deeper understanding of history and heritage, and allow you to effortlessly integrate historical information within music instruction. *Teaching Music Across History* is not only necessary, but FUN!

---

* *National Standards for Music Education.* Copyright © 1994 by National Association for Music Education (NAfME). Used by permission. The complete national arts standards and additional materials relating to the standards are available from NAfME, 1806 Robert Fulton Drive, Reston, VA 20191.

NATIONAL MUSIC STANDARD 9

Great-Great-Great Inventions!

★ **Overview of Music History Time Periods**

Time Needed:
Approximately 30 minutes

Objective:
Students will be given an overview of the dates and innovations of the Baroque, Classical, Romantic, and Modern musical time periods.

Resources Needed:
✂ Student worksheets
✂ Pencils
✂ Art supplies (if available)

Lesson:
1. Discuss the meaning of "ancestors."
    ♪ An ancestor is a person from whom you are directly descended, especially someone more distant than a grandparent.

2. Describe how music is divided into time periods.
    ♪ Baroque music (1600–1750) had decorated and fancy melodies.
    ♪ Classical music (1750–1825) was more simple and balanced.
    ♪ Romantic music (1825–1900) expressed greater passion.
    ♪ Modern music (1900–the present) includes jazz, rock 'n' roll, and electronic music.

3. Pass out the invention sheets and read the directions aloud.

4. Students can work individually or in pairs.
    ♪ Encourage artistic work.
    ♪ Answers and cartoons may vary.

Teaching Music Across History

Below are lists of inventions created during the musical time periods "Baroque," "Classical," "Romantic," and "Modern." Choose one invention and write a sentence about how your ancestor may have used it. Then, create a drawing of the event.

Baroque Period Inventions (1600–1750)

(Music of this period had decorated and fancy melodies.)

INVENTION	YEAR	INVENTOR	COUNTRY
Telescope, optical	1608	Hans Lippershey	The Netherlands
Submarine	1620	Cornelis Drebbel	The Netherlands
Clock, pendulum	1656	Christiaan Huygens	The Netherlands
Engine, steam	1698	Thomas Savery	England

Classical Period Inventions (1750–1825)

(Music of the period was more simple and balanced.)

INVENTION	YEAR	INVENTOR	COUNTRY
Sunglasses	1752	James Ayscough	U.K.
Soft drinks, carbonation	1772	Joseph Priestley	U.K.
Balloon, hot-air	1783	Joseph & Étienne Montgolfier	France
Oil lamp	1784	Aimé Argand	Switzerland
Shoelaces	1790	unknown	England
Cotton gin	1793	Eli Whitney	U.S.
Vaccination	1796	Edward Jenner	England
Parachute, modern	1797	André-Jacques Garnerin	France
Canning, food	1809	Nicolas Appert	France
American Sign Language	1817	Thomas H. Gallaudet	U.S.
Bicycle	1818	Baron Karl de Drais de Sauerbrun	Germany
Stethoscope	1819	René-Théophile-Hyacinthe Laënnec	France

Romantic Period Inventions (1825–1900)

(Music of this period expressed greater passion.)

INVENTION	YEAR	INVENTOR	COUNTRY
Braille system	1824	Louis Braille	France
Motor, electric	1834	Thomas Davenport	U.S.
Photography	1837	Louis-Jacques-Mandé Daguerre	France
Morse code	1838	Samuel F.B. Morse	U.S.
Refrigerator	1842	John Gorrie	U.S.
Rubber band	1845	Stephen Perry	U.K.
Saxophone	1846	Antoine-Joseph Sax	Belgium
Safety pin	1849	Walter Hunt	U.S.
Elevator, passenger	1852	Elisha Graves Otis	U.S.
Potato chips	1853	George Crum	U.S.
Stapler	1866	George W. McGill	U.S.
Dynamite	1867	Alfred Nobel	Sweden
Typewriter	1868	Christopher Latham Sholes	U.S.
Telephone, wired-line	1876	Alexander Graham Bell	Scotland/Canada/US
Phonograph	1877	Thomas Alva Edison	U.S.
Roller coaster	1884	LeMarcus A. Thompson	U.S.
Motorcycle	1885	Gottlieb Daimler, Wilhelm Maybach	Germany
Contact lenses	1887	Adolf Fick	Germany
Camera, portable photographic	1888	George Eastman	U.S.
Door, revolving	1888	Theophilus von Kannel	U.S.
Straw, drinking	1888	Marvin Stone	U.S.
Automobile	1889	Gottlieb Daimler	Germany
Jukebox	1889	Louis Glass	U.S.

Teaching Music Across History

Modern Period Inventions (1900–Present)

(Music of this period includes jazz, rock 'n' roll, and electronic music.)

INVENTION	YEAR	INVENTOR	COUNTRY
Vacuum cleaner, electric	1901	Herbert Cecil Booth	U.K.
Airplane, engine-powered	1903	Wilbur and Orville Wright	U.S.
Washing machine, electric	1907	Alva J. Fisher	U.S.
Neon lighting	1910	Georges Claude	France
Assembly line	1913	Henry Ford	U.S.
Crossword puzzles	1913	Arthur Wynne	U.S.
Polygraph (lie detector)	1921	John A. Larson	U.S.
Snowmobile	1922	Joseph-Armand Bombardier	Canada
Traffic lights, automatic	1923	Garrett A. Morgan	U.S.
Razor, electric	1928	Jacob Schick	U.S.
Monopoly (board game)	1934	Charles B. Darrow	U.S.
Helicopter	1939	Igor Sikorsky	Russia/U.S.
Guitar, electric	1941	Les Paul	U.S.
Nuclear reactor	1942	Enrico Fermi	U.S.
Scuba gear	1943	Jacques Cousteau, Émile Gagnan	France
Sunscreen	1944	Benjamin Green	U.S.
Microwave oven	1945	Percy L. Spencer	U.S.
Credit card	1950	Frank McNamara, Ralph Schneider (Diners' Club)	U.S.
Remote control, television	1950	Robert Adler	U.S.

Student Name: _____

Directions: Describe an invention your ancestors would have used during each of the music history periods. Create drawings of each invention you choose.

My great-great-great-great-great-great-great-great-grandfather was born in 1710, during the Baroque period (1600–1750). He _____

_____

_____

My great-great-great-great-great-great-grandfather was born in 1770, during the Classical period (1750–1825). He _____

_____

_____

Teaching Music Across History

My great-great-grandfather was born in 1890, during the Romantic period (1825–1900).

He _____

_____

_____

My grandfather was born in 1950, during the Modern period (1900–present day). He _____

_____

_____

_____

Teaching Music Across History

NATIONAL MUSIC STANDARD 9

Holiday Fun

★ **Federal Holiday Music**

Time Needed:
Approximately 30 minutes

Objective:
Students will be given a brief overview of the music that correlates to the federal holidays celebrated in the United States.

Resources Needed:
✂ Student worksheets
✂ Pencils

Lesson:
1. As an anticipatory set, ask the students what their favorite holidays are. Responses will vary.
2. Tell the students there are 11 federal holidays. As a class, list the holidays (and *not* their accompanying songs) on the board. They will determine what the songs are when they complete the worksheets.
   - ♪ New Year's Day—"Auld Lang Syne"
   - ♪ Inauguration Day—"Hail to the Chief"
   - ♪ The Birthday of Martin Luther King, Jr.—"We Shall Overcome"
   - ♪ Washington's Birthday—"Yankee Doodle"
   - ♪ Memorial Day—"Taps"
   - ♪ Independence Day—"The Star-Spangled Banner"
   - ♪ Labor Day—"I've Been Working on the Railroad"
   - ♪ Columbus Day—"America"
   - ♪ Veteran's Day—"The Army Goes Rolling Along," "Anchors Aweigh," "Marine's Hymn," "Wild Blue Yonder," "Semper Paratus" (Always Ready)
   - ♪ Thanksgiving Day—"Over the River and Through the Wood"
   - ♪ Christmas—"White Christmas"
3. Instruct the students to read through the descriptions of the holidays and the holiday songs on their worksheet. Ask them to fill in the blanks based on the clues given in each section. The songs are listed above.
4. Students can work individually or in pairs.
5. Check and review the answers when completed.

Teaching Music Across History

Student Name: _____

Fill in the blanks below using the answers found in the grid below.

Holidays

Fun! Fun! Fun!

Everyone loves holidays! They're a time for celebrating and honoring important events and people. Using your knowledge of these beloved dates, insert the words from the list of holidays and their related songs to complete the story below. (Hint: the songs have quotation marks at the beginning and end of the titles.) The first one is done for you.

Washington's Birthday	"Yankee Doodle"
Independence Day	"The Star-Spangled Banner"
New Year's Day ✓	"Auld Lang Syne" ✓
Inauguration Day	"Hail to the Chief"
Christmas	"White Christmas"
Veteran's Day	"The Army Goes Rolling Along" "Anchors Aweigh" "Marine's Hymn" "Wild Blue Yonder" "Semper Paratus" (Always Ready)
Columbus Day	"America"
Labor Day	"I've Been Working on the Railroad"
Birthday of Martin Luther King, Jr.	"We Shall Overcome"
Thanksgiving Day	"Over the River and Through the Woods"
Memorial Day	"Taps"

Teaching Music Across History

1. Did you know there are 11 United States Federal holidays? The first holiday we commemorate every year is called <u>New Year's Day</u> and occurs on January 1st. We celebrate the beginning of the Gregorian calendar year on this day, but often begin the festivities the evening before by counting down the time until midnight. People often wear silly hats, blow horns, and throw confetti during the event. A poem called "<u>Auld Lang Syne</u>," written by Robert Burns in 1788, was set to a familiar folk song and is commonly sung on this day. The three words in the title literally mean, "times long past."

2. This holiday, _____, occurs after the presidential election every fourth year, when the president is sworn into office on January 20th. A famous march, titled

   _____,

   is often played to announce the arrival of the president of our country. Sir Walter Scott wrote the lyrics, which were set to music in the early 1800s. This famous march was first played for the commemoration of George Washington's birthday in 1815. During President Truman's administration, the Department of Defense declared it to be the official tribute to our presidents. (Did you know the wife of one of our earlier presidents wanted this music played every time her husband entered a formal event, because he was so plain-looking that people often overlooked his attendance, which she found to be quite embarrassing? Want to know who it was? President Polk.)

3. The next federal holiday of the year falls on the third Monday in January. This special holiday,

   _____,

   celebrates the birth of a famous African American civil rights leader who was born on January 15, 1929. He is well known for his speech called, "I Have a Dream." He often used the words in the song

   _____,

   in his speeches. The song is a combination of an African American spiritual and a hymn, and was one of the most popular civil rights songs in the 1960s.

Teaching Music Across History

4. The following holiday, _____,
falls on the third Monday in February. On this day we celebrate another famous person's birthday, who was born on February 22, 1732. He was the commander in chief of the Continental army during the American Revolution. He assisted with the writing of the Constitution and became the first President of the United States. He is known as the father of our country. A song that was very popular during this time was called

_____,

The lyrics to this folk song were actually composed during the French and Indian War during the 1750s. The British wanted to make fun of the American soldiers and the uniforms they wore. The Americans were amused and wrote different versions of the song, which we still sing today.

5. On this holiday, which occurs on the last Monday in May, we remember both family members and military service men and women who have died. Out of respect, it is a common practice to place flowers, or other sentimental items, on their grave sites. This holiday,

_____,

was originally started to honor the soldiers who had died in the Civil War, but was later extended to Americans who had passed away in any war. A common melody that is performed at the wreath ceremonies in the Arlington National Cemetery is called

_____.

This simple melody uses a combination of four different pitches to create the haunting melody which is often played on a bugle.

6. One of America's favorite holidays, which falls on the fourth of July, is called

_____.

This colorful holiday is celebrated with fireworks, barbecues, and laughter! The holiday actually commemorates the signing of the Declaration of Independence in 1776, which resulted in Americans fighting to gain their freedom from Britain. Over 30 years later, Francis Scott Key wrote a poem about a battle he observed during the War of 1812 between the British Royal Navy ships and our military stationed at Fort McHenry. The words were set to a lively British tune written by John Stafford Smith, and the song was named

_____.

On March 3, 1931, President Herbert Hoover declared this song to be our national anthem. Today this anthem is so popular it is sung for many patriotic celebrations.

7. On the first Monday in September, we celebrate this federal holiday known as

_____,

in honor of the working men and women in the United States. This day was declared a national holiday in 1878, following a conflict between the labor unions and the railroad workers during the Pullman Strike. A popular song called

_____,

would be appropriate to sing on this day because it describes the toils of railroad workers. There appears to be some question about the origin of this melody. Some believe it came from a levee song by African Americans, while others believe it originated with the Irish work gangs of the wild West.

8. In 1492, this man sailed the ocean blue. The holiday,

_____,

is officially celebrated on the second Monday in October in honor of this famous Italian explorer who landed in the Bahamas on October 12, 1492. His four sailing expeditions to the New World brought new awareness of the area to the Europeans. President Franklin Delano Roosevelt officially declared this day a federal holiday in 1934. A patriotic song titled

_____,

has the same name as the western continents in the area he explored. The lyrics to this song were actually written on a scrap piece of paper salvaged from the trash can by Samuel Francis Smith in 1831. One of his friends had sent him several German hymnals. When he found a patriotic German hymn in one of the books, he suddenly had the desire to write one for his country. In approximately 30 minutes, he completed the lyrics which he set to a British melody.

Teaching Music Across History

9. This holiday, _____,
is sometimes called Armistice Day. It is celebrated on November 11th and honors the signing of the armistice at the end of World War I. All veterans from every branch are honored whether they served during wartime or not. There are five branches of armed services in the United States today. Each one has their own song.
The Army's song is called:

_____,

the Navy's song is called:

_____,

the Marines' song is called:

_____,

the name of the song for the Air Force is:

_____,

and the name of the Coast Guard song is:

_____.

10. Once a year on the fourth Thursday in November, many families gather together to enjoy a turkey dinner complete with all the "fixings," which is called

_____.

This tradition first began when the pilgrims shared food with the Native Americans in their area. A popular song that is often performed in conjunction with this holiday is called

_____.

People often think this is a Christmas song, but the lyrics in the second verse prove this to be wrong. The words refer to this holiday twice, and mention pumpkin pie. Lydia Maria Child originally wrote the lyrics of this song as a poem, published in 1844, to capture her memories of visiting her grandfather's house on this special day.

11. The last federal holiday of the year falls on December 25th and is called

_____.

This religious holiday is celebrated both in the states and abroad. Many people exchange gifts, and display elaborate festive decorations at this time. Ulysses S. Grant declared this to be a federal holiday in 1870. There is a score of songs sung around this holiday, but one of the standards is called

_____.

Irving Berlin wrote this song in the early 1940s, and it has sold millions of copies. The song describes a snowy, old-fashioned holiday.

Teaching Music Across History

NATIONAL MUSIC STANDARD 9

The Pledge of Allegiance

★ **Brief Historic Background of the Pledge of Allegiance**

Time Needed:
Approximately 30 to 40 minutes

Objective:
Using the pre-review sheet and both the original and current versions of the **Pledge of Allegiance**, the students will gain an understanding of the meaning and origin of our country's pledge.

Resources Needed:
- Student pre-test
- Pencils
- Original and current copy of the Pledge of Allegiance
- Time line sheet
- Optional: patriotic music

Lesson:
1. As an anticipatory set, recite the Pledge of Allegiance.
2. Instruct the students to take a fun test based on their knowledge of the Pledge of Allegiance.
3. Upon completion of the test, review the answers as a class.
   - D. Francis Bellamy
   - B. 1892
   - A. The 400 year anniversary of Columbus Day
   - A. Shorter—only 23 words long
   - B. A promise
   - A. To support or be loyal to something or someone
   - C. A government in which the leaders are elected by the people
   - C. Something that can't be divided
   - D. All of the above
   - E. All answers except D
   - C. Symbolizes the loyalty we feel for our country and is said out of respect by those who choose to take part in reciting the words
4. Instruct the students to identify the differences between the original Pledge of Allegiance and the pledge we use today as depicted on the time line.
5. Teach or review a few patriotic songs to tie in with this unit. For example, sing the first verse of "America." Then repeat, instructing half the class to sing the melody of "America" using "ooh" instead of the lyrics, while the other half recites the words of the Pledge of Allegiance.

Teaching Music Across History

Student Name: _____

The Pledge of Allegiance

Traditionally, many students begin their school day by reciting the Pledge of Allegiance. Often the words are simply chanted without giving much thought to their true meaning. Below is a short quiz to test your knowledge of the origin and meaning of our country's pledge.

1. The Pledge of Allegiance was written by:

    A. George Washington

    B. Justin Bieber

    C. Thomas Edison

    D. Francis Bellamy

2. The Pledge of Allegiance was written in:

    A. 1492

    B. 1892

    C. 1776

    D. 2059

3. The pledge was written in honor of:

    A. The 400 year anniversary of Columbus Day

    B. Saint Nicholas

    C. Veterans who served in World War I and II

    D. Earth Day

4. The original pledge was:

    A. Shorter—only 23 words long

    B. Longer—120 words long

    C. The same—31 words long

    D. None of the above

5. The definition of a pledge is:

    A. A citizen

    B. A promise

    C. Someone who works for the government

    D. A secret code

6. "Allegiance" means:

    A. To support or be loyal to something or someone

    B. You have betrayed someone's trust

    C. You have been convicted of a crime

    D. You're married

Teaching Music Across History

7. The term "republic" means:

    A. A popular brand of jeans

    B. A government ruled by a king and/or a queen

    C. A government in which the leaders are elected by the people

    D. A dictatorship

8. The definition of the word "indivisible" is:

    A. Something you can't see

    B. The visible stripes on a tiger

    C. Something that can't be divided

    D. Something that can be divided

9. The pledge is often said:

    A. At the beginning of the school day

    B. At a Scout meeting

    C. At official meetings

    D. All of the above

    E. None of the above

10. When saying the pledge, it is proper to:

    A. Stand and face the flag

    B. Place your right hand over your heart

    C. Remove your hat unless you are in the military, then place your hat over your heart

    D. Hop on one foot

    E. All answers except D

11. The Pledge of Allegiance:

    A. Is a law that must be obeyed

    B. Must be said by everyone

    C. Symbolizes the loyalty we feel for our country and is said out of respect by those who choose to take part in reciting the words

    D. Is only recited when outside

Teaching Music Across History

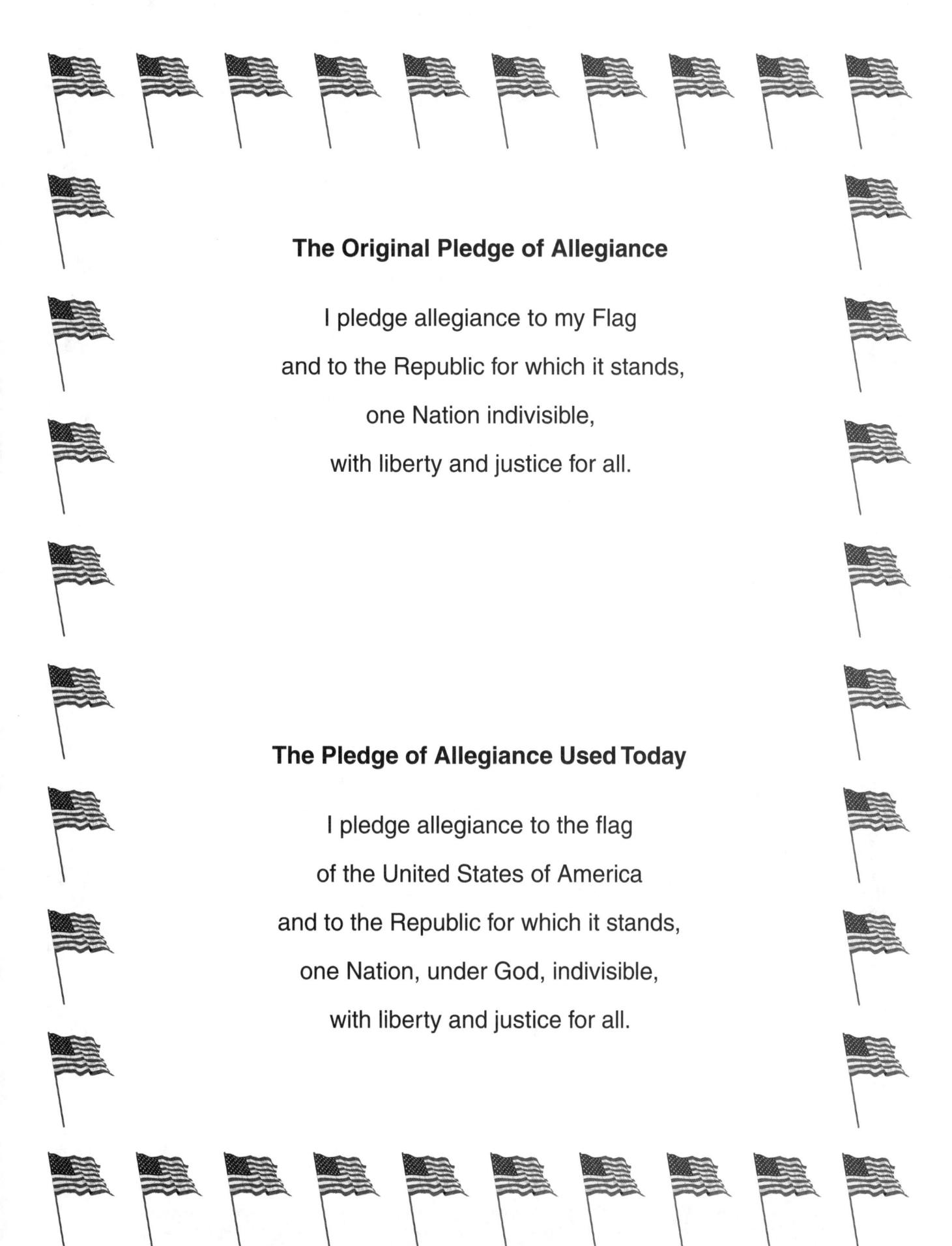

The Original Pledge of Allegiance

I pledge allegiance to my Flag

and to the Republic for which it stands,

one Nation indivisible,

with liberty and justice for all.

The Pledge of Allegiance Used Today

I pledge allegiance to the flag

of the United States of America

and to the Republic for which it stands,

one Nation, under God, indivisible,

with liberty and justice for all.

Teaching Music Across History

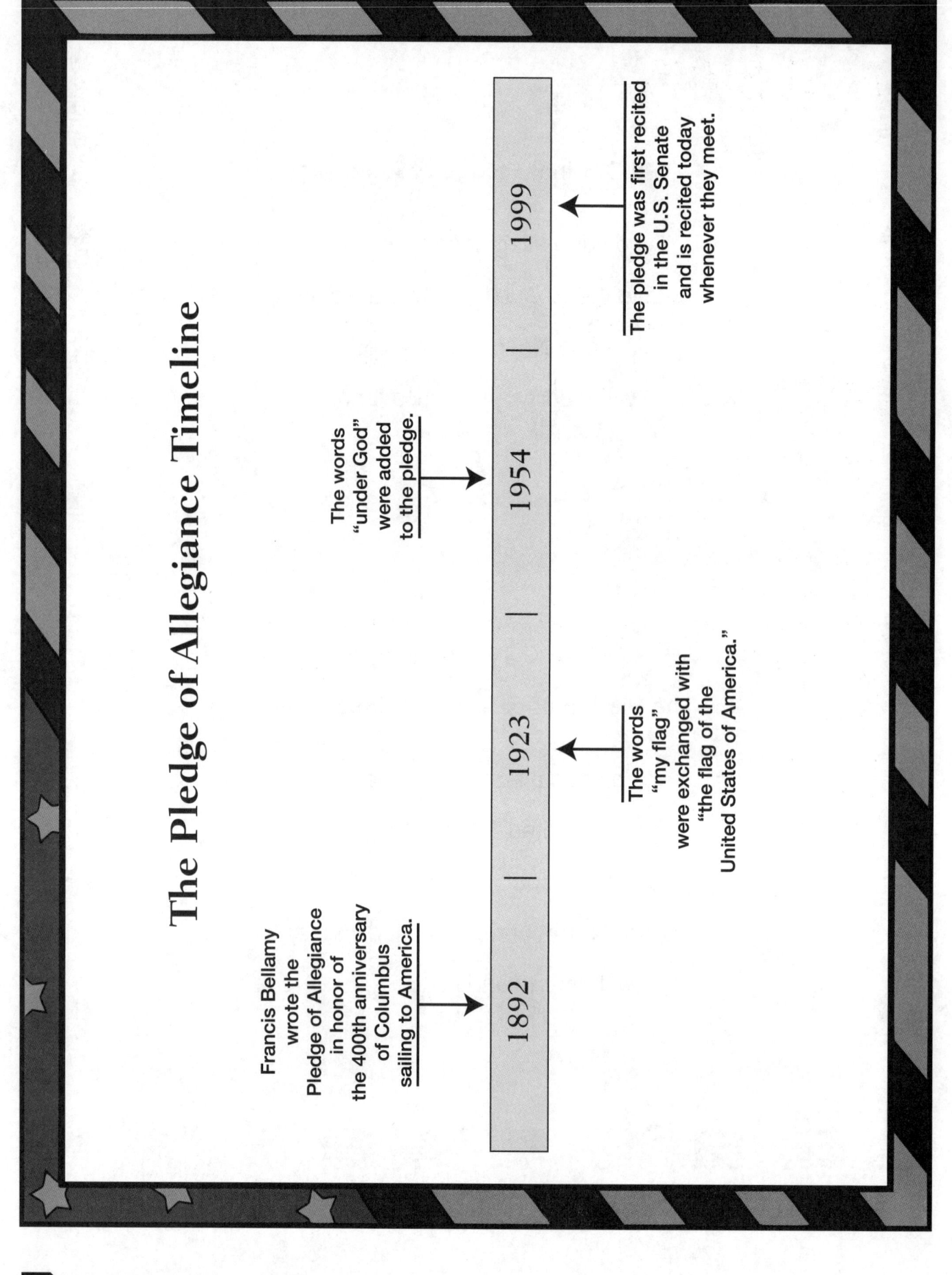

The Pledge of Allegiance Timeline

1892 — Francis Bellamy wrote the Pledge of Allegiance in honor of the 400th anniversary of Columbus sailing to America.

1923 — The words "my flag" were exchanged with "the flag of the United States of America."

1954 — The words "under God" were added to the pledge.

1999 — The pledge was first recited in the U.S. Senate and is recited today whenever they meet.

Teaching Music Across History

NATIONAL MUSIC STANDARD 9

String Story

Time Needed:
Approximately 30 minutes

Objective:
Using a worksheet and listening selection, students will explore the history of the violin. (This lesson may be used as promotion for your school's string program.)

Resources Needed:
- CD ("Badinerie")
- CD player
- Student worksheets
- Pencils

Lesson:
1. Pass out *History of the Violin*.
2. Read the sheet aloud.
3. Pass out the rebec/violin worksheet. (It can be printed on the back of the history sheet.)
4. Play the music "Badinerie," by Corelli while students compare the rebec and violin.
5. **Answer Key**

    The rebec and the violin are different because the rebec doesn't have:
    - ♪ <u>Chin rest</u>
    - ♪ <u>Fine tuners</u>
    - ♪ <u>Four strings</u>
    - ♪ <u>Waist (C bout)</u>

Teaching Music Across History

History of the Violin

Once upon a time (around the 9th century), an instrument craftsman pulled an "arched bow" (like you would use for a bow and arrow) over a stringed instrument and created an interesting sound.

The rebec was played under the chin, like a violin, and was developed in southern Europe in the Middle Ages, inspired by the "rebab" and similar instruments introduced to Europe by Muslim merchants and artists from Arab countries. The four strings and the f-holes were forerunners of the future violin. Some instruments were played by holding them against the left shoulder, while some were played resting on the performer's knee.

At first, some of the stringed instruments had one string, then two, then three, then four. Slowly the stringed instrument of the Middle Ages changed from having a round opening (like an acoustic guitar) to having two curve-shaped holes.

Rebec

During the Renaissance period (approximately 1300–1600), one of the major stringed instruments was the viola da braccio, which was held against the shoulder. Stringed instrument names are all derived from the word viola, taken from the Latin word vitula, meaning "stringed instrument." The violin was first "born" in the 1600s.

One of the composers who mastered this new instrument and composed great music for the violin was Arcangelo Corelli, who was born in 1653, during the Baroque period (approximately 1600–1750).

Student Name: _____

What's the Difference?

Listen to the "**Badinerie**," a dance written by Corelli, while you identify the differences between the **rebec** and the **violin**. Its name comes from the French word for "***jesting***" or "***joking***."

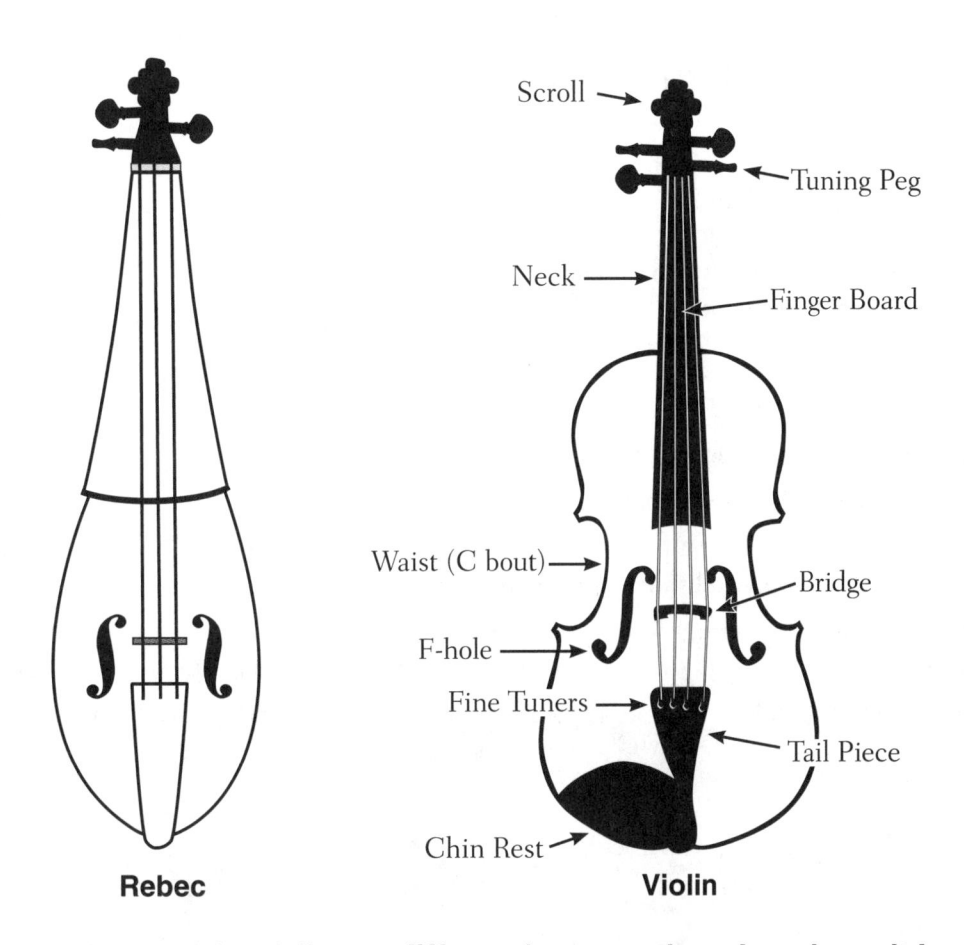

Rebec

Violin

Labels on violin: Scroll, Tuning Peg, Neck, Finger Board, Waist (C bout), Bridge, F-hole, Fine Tuners, Tail Piece, Chin Rest

The rebec and the violin are *different* because *the rebec doesn't have*:

1. _____

2. _____

3. _____

4. _____

The violin is a great instrument to learn! *And that's no "badinerie" (joke)!*

Teaching Music Across History

NATIONAL MUSIC STANDARD 9

Forward March

Time Needed:
Approximately 30 minutes

Objective:
The students will explore the history of the marching band.

Resources Needed:
- Forward March (marching band history)
- Student quiz sheet and paper doll
- Art supplies (colored pencils, crayons, scissors)
- CD Bizet's March—"Trumpet and Drum," "Impromptu" (*Jeux D'Enfants*)
- *Optional: display a photograph of a local university's marching band*

Lesson::

1. Pass out student sheet ("Forward March").

2. Read aloud the history of the marching band.

   ♪ Popcorn reading: read the first paragraph and stop abruptly, having the entire class say the next missing word. (This is an additional tool to keep students' attention on the text.)

   ♪ Take turns reading each paragraph, allowing students to be the readers. (This will give weaker readers the chance to stop on difficult words, while the entire class fills in the blank).

3. After reading the section about the drum and bugle, sing the A section of this bugle call to your students (ta, ta …):

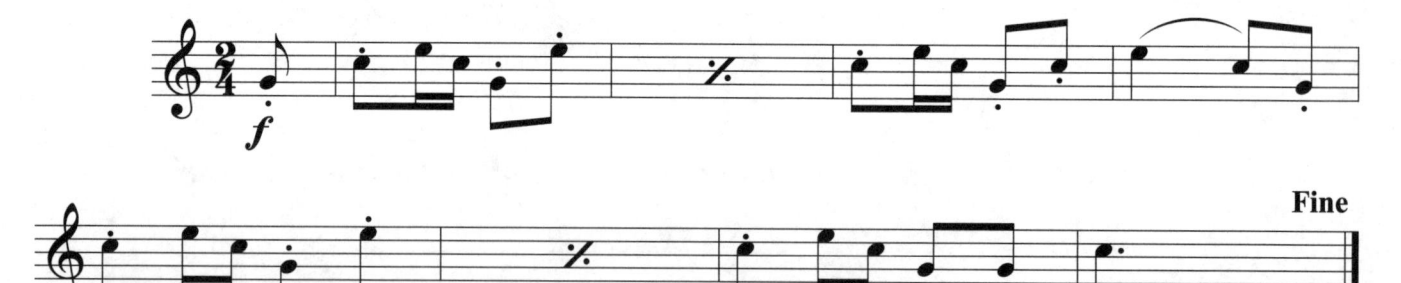

4. Some students will recognize this as "*Reveille*," which signals the troops to awaken for morning roll call. "Reveille" is also used to accompany the raising of the national colors. (This is a good example of how the bugle is used for commands.)

5. Pass out student quiz. (Alternatively, you could have the quiz printed on the back of Forward March.)

24 Teaching Music Across History

6. Students will answer three questions (the answers are below in **bold**):

    1. What is the date for the earliest fife and drum band?

        a. **1291 (the Swiss army)**

        b. 1775 (the American colonists)

        c. 1861 (the Union army)

    2. Marching bands were used with military bands to:

        a. Help soldiers march to the beat

        b. Lift soldiers' spirits

        c. Boost a sense of pride (patriotism)

        d. **All of the above**

    3. True or false? High school bands use similar direction as military bands. **True**
        - ♪ *Optional: display a photograph of one of your state's university marching bands.*
            - *Point out the significant design elements of their uniforms.*
        - ♪ *Pass out the marching band doll. Students will design a military-style band uniform while listening to Bizet's March—"Trumpet and Drum," "Impromptu" (Jeux D'Enfants)*
            - *Optional: students can cut out their paper doll and it can be used on a marching band bulletin board.*

Forward March

If you've ever been to a parade, or a high school or college football game, you've seen a marching band. Marching bands generally perform outdoors and consist of brass, woodwind, and percussion instruments.

Marching bands have been around as long as soldiers have had instruments. Drums were used to help groups of military men and women march together and could be heard by a large group of marchers. Adding a melody along with the beat helped lift the soldiers' spirits and gave them a sense of pride and patriotism.

The common combination of musical instruments changed during each period, probably due to the instruments that were available. The Swiss army used the fife and drum in 1291, and then many of the other European armies adopted that style in their military bands. Colonists were just doing what was popular at the time. Fife and drums were used during the American Revolutionary War. The Revolutionary War was fought during 1775–83, when the 13 colonies joined together against British rule in America.

Throughout the American Civil War, drum and bugle corps were mainly used. Drums and bugles communicated commands to the soldiers and officers. The American Civil War was fought in 1861–1865, when 11 southern states left the group of states governed by the federal government and formed The Confederate States of America. The remaining 25 northern states were called "the Union."

In the 20th Century, American brass, woodwind, and percussion military bands played during World War I (1914–1918) and World War II (1939–45). Drum and bugle commands were eventually replaced by modern communication, but the bands remain as a tradition and patriotic symbol of military life.

The next time you go to a parade or a high school or college football game, notice that these bands still follow military directions, such as being called to "attention," "about face," and "forward march." They also wear uniforms that still look like those used in the military.

School marching bands, like military marching bands, help to boost pride in their organization and are a very important part of every high school! *Learn to play an instrument and join the band!*

Student Name: _____

Test your knowledge (circle your answer):

1. What is the date for the earliest fife and drum band?

   a. 1291 (the Swiss army)

   b. 1775 (the American colonists)

   c. 1861 (the Union army)

2. Marching bands were used with the military to:

   a. Help soldiers march to the beat

   b. Lift soldiers' spirits

   c. Boost a sense of pride (patriotism)

   d. All of the above

3. True or false? High school bands use similar direction as military bands.

   _____

Student Name: _____

Below, design a uniform for your marching band member. Remember to use a military style.

28 Teaching Music Across History

NATIONAL MUSIC STANDARD 9

Compacting Composers

Time Needed:
Approximately 30 minutes

Objective:
Students will practice summarization while using composer biographies.

Resources Needed:
- Student practice sheet
- (Bizet)
- Corelli biography worksheet
- CD (*Jeux d'enfants* —"Trumpet and Drum," "Impromptu," and "Badinerie")
- Pencils
- CD player

Lesson:
1. Pass out the student practice sheet (Bizet biography) and explain, "Today, we're going to practice SUMMARIZATION, a very important skill you can use for the rest of your life in any subject area and at any grade level."

2. The three keys to summarization:

   ♪ **Retain** (Keep anything really important, including topic sentences and other really important information—don't keep EVERYTHING!) Making decisions on what is truly important may be difficult for some students.

       a. Keep the "*who*," "*what*," or "*where*" (the subject of the paragraph/article).

       b. Keep the *most* important information about that subject.

   ♪ **Remove**

       a. Take away less important information.

       b. Look for information that isn't absolutely necessary to understanding the subject.

   ♪ **Replace**

       a. Substitute a category word for a list of information. For example, the statement "This composer wrote 3 operas, 7 symphonies, 4 string quartets, and 10 sonatas" could be summarized as "This composer wrote many types of music."

3. Read Bizet's biography as a group, modeling the logic behind the summarization of the information.

Teaching Music Across History

4. **Answer Key**

Georges Bizet

Georges Bizet was born in ~~Paris,~~ France ~~on October 25, 1838. His parents were musicians, and encouraged him to become a musician. Georges loved playing and writing music, but he also loved to read books so much that his parents hid them so he would spend less time reading and more time practicing. He began studying at the Paris Conservatory when he was 10 years old, where he wrote his only symphony. After graduation, he began writing operas.~~

Bizet ~~was a great pianist, but~~ preferred to write operas, ~~such as Les pêcheurs de perles, La jolie fille de Perth, Djamileh,~~ and Carmen, Bizet's most famous work, ~~even though when it was first performed the critics didn't like it. (They wrongly said Carmen had no great melodies, so the audiences avoided spending their money to see it.) He died shortly after that opera premiered, at the age of 36 of a heart attack, on June 3, 1875. Later that year, Carmen opened in Vienna, Austria, where the audiences loved it! Too bad Bizet never knew~~ Carmen would be considered a masterpiece and become one of the most widely performed operas in the world.

Summary: Georges Bizet was a French composer, who preferred to write operas. Carmen, Bizet's most famous work, would be considered a masterpiece and become one of the most widely performed operas in the world.

- ♪ The most important "who" is Georges Bizet.
- ♪ The most important "what" is his opera, *Carmen*.
- ♪ He was a composer who wrote operas.
- ♪ Your students' summaries may vary slightly, but keep in mind: the important skill is for students to evaluate the information.

5. After the students have read and discussed the first summarization, let them work independently on the second summarization.

6. If students have questions, provide feedback, including:
   - ♪ Who are we talking about (*the subject*).
   - ♪ Can you identify the "topic sentence" (usually the first sentence in a paragraph)?
   - ♪ Is that information REALLY important to understanding the composer's life?
   - ♪ Look for a list of musical compositions and replace the list with phrases like "many types of music," "vocal music," "instrumental music," etc.

7. Continue practice with Corelli's biography.

8. **Answer Key** (answers may vary).

   Arcangelo Corelli

   Arcangelo Corelli was ~~born on February 17, 1653 in Italy and became~~ a famous violinist and composer in the Baroque musical period. ~~His first violin lessons were given to him by a local priest and his first composition lessons were given to him by Matteo Simonelli, a famous singer of the pope's chapel.~~

   Corelli was the most important violinist of his time. ~~He introduced a beautiful style called "Cantabile," or songlike, playing, and was the teacher of other famous violinist/composers including George Frederick Handel and Antonio Vivaldi.~~

   As a composer, Corelli chose to write music for stringed instruments using major and minor tonalities, ~~rather than the modes from the church. His playing and compositions were very well respected and he died a wealthy man on January 8, 1713.~~

   Summary: Arcangelo Corelli was a famous violinist and composer in the Baroque musical period and was the most important violinist of his time. As a composer, Corelli chose to write music for stringed instruments using major and minor tonalities.

9. After the class has completed their summarizations, read selected student summarizations aloud with the corresponding compositions as a soundtrack.

   ♪ Bizet: March—"Trumpet and Drum," "Impromptu," or "The Top" (*Jeux d'enfants*)

   ♪ Corelli: *Badinerie*

10. For even more practice, use Jay Althouse's *One-Page Composer Bios: 50 Reproducible Biographies of Famous Composers*. That book also includes biographies of composers featured on the CD included with this book:

    ♪ Grieg

    ♪ Mendelssohn

    ♪ Mozart

    ♪ Tchaikovsky

Compacting Composers

Being able to "summarize" what you've read is a skill you'll use for the rest of your educational career. You will be called upon to summarize in written tests, when you take notes for classes, even when you're retelling the plot of a movie to your friends.

One successful summarizing strategy is to **RETAIN, REMOVE**, and **REPLACE** information.

1. **Retain**

    a. Keep the *"who," "what,"* or *"where."*

    b. Keep the *most* important information about that subject.

2. **Remove** (Take away less important information. Look for information that isn't absolutely necessary to understand the subject.)

3. **Replace** (Insert a category word for a list of information. For example, the statement "This composer wrote **3 operas, 7 symphonies, 4 string quartets, and 10 sonatas**" could be summarized as "This composer wrote **many types of music**.")

Read the following biography and as a group, *retain* the "who," "what," and "where" or subjects. ***Remove*** all information that isn't about the *"who," "what,"* and *"where"* by placing a light line through any information. Finally, *replace* any lists of information with a topic or category word.

Teaching Music Across History

Student Name: _____

Georges Bizet

Georges Bizet was born in Paris, France on October 25, 1838. His parents were musicians, and encouraged him to become a musician. Georges loved playing and writing music, but he also loved to read books so much that his parents hid them so he would spend less time reading and more time practicing. He began studying at the Paris Conservatory when he was 10 years old, where he wrote his only symphony. After graduation, he began writing operas.

Bizet was a great pianist, but preferred to write operas, such as *Les pêcheurs de perles, La jolie fille de Perth, Djamileh*, and *Carmen*, Bizet's most famous work, even though when it was first performed the critics didn't like it. (They wrongly said Carmen had no great melodies, so the audiences avoided spending their money to see it.) He died shortly after that opera premiered, at the age of 36 of a heart attack, on June 3, 1875. Later that year, Carmen opened in Vienna, Austria, where the audiences loved it! Too bad Bizet never knew Carmen would be considered a masterpiece and become one of the most widely performed operas in the world.

Write a summary:

_____

_____

_____

_____

_____

Teaching Music Across History

Arcangelo Corelli

Arcangelo Corelli was born on February 17, 1653 in Italy and became a famous violinist and composer in the baroque musical period. His first violin lessons were given to him by a local priest and his first composition lessons were given to him by Matteo Simonelli, a famous singer of the pope's chapel.

Corelli was the most important violinist of his time. He introduced a beautiful style called "Cantabile," or *songlike*, playing and was the teacher of other famous violinist/composers including George Frederick Handel and Antonio Vivaldi.

As a composer, Corelli chose to write music for stringed instruments using major and minor tonalities, rather than the modes from the church. His playing and composition were very well respected and he died a wealthy man on January 8, 1713.

Write a summary:

_____

_____

_____

_____

_____

Crack the Code

NATIONAL MUSIC STANDARD 9

Time Needed:
Approximately 30 minutes

Objective:
Students solve math word problems, indicating changes in the orchestra throughout four musical periods (Baroque–Modern).

Resources Needed:
- Pencils
- CD
    - *Badinerie* (Corelli)
    - *Minuet* (Mozart)
    - *In the Hall of the Mountain King* (Grieg)
    - *A Lincoln Portrait* (Copland)
- Student sheets
- Colored pencils/crayons optional

For each student, a copy of each period's currency (four, total). See pages 39 and 40.

Lesson:
1. Pass out the student sheets and pencils.
2. Read and discuss the directions.
    - Students will solve math questions using historical information.
    - Students should write their answers in the spaces provided.
3. Students will work independently (or in small groups, if necessary) to solve the questions and "crack the code."
4. **Answer Key**

    A. How many total string players are in a Baroque orchestra? _19_

    B. How many total string players are in a Modern orchestra? _61_

    C. How many woodwind players are in the Classical orchestra? _8_

    D. How many more woodwind players were added to the Romantic orchestra? _6_

    E. How many more total instruments were in the Romantic than the Baroque orchestra? _72_

Teaching Music Across History

5. *After* the students have solved the word problems, tell them it's time they receive their reward.
   - ♪ Each student will receive one of each of the period's currencies.
     A. Picture of a composer (who will serve as the treasurer for that period).
     B. The total number of instruments used in the period's orchestra is the number on the currency.
     C. If you have time, let the students decorate/color the currencies.

6. Play the following excerpts to demonstrate the sound of the orchestras while passing out the currency and/or coloring each.
   - ♪ Baroque: *Badinerie* (Corelli)
   - ♪ Classical: *Minuet* (Mozart)
   - ♪ Romantic: *In the Hall of the Mountain King* (Grieg)
   - ♪ Modern: *A Lincoln Portrait* (Copland)

7. For a technology connection and to show pictures of the instruments, visit the following site:

artsedge.kennedy-center.org/interactives/perfectpitch/

Student Name: _____

Crack the Code

A strange musician, historian, and philanthropist, J.P. Money, left a safe full of cash to your elementary school's music department. The only problem: Mr. Money left the safe's combination in a *secret code*. The code can be solved by using knowledge about the orchestra's size in different musical time periods. The school's music teacher was able to gather the necessary information, but we need YOU to read the clues and **crack the code**.

Here's what you need to know.

The Baroque orchestra (1600–1750) generally used these instruments:

Strings	Woodwind	Brass	Keyboard	Percussion
Violin I (6)	Flute (2)	Horns (2)	Harpsichord(1)	Timpani (1)
Violin 2 (6)	Oboe (2)	Trumpets (2)		
Viola (4)	Bassoon (2)			
Cello (2)				
Bass (1)				

The Classical orchestra (1750–1825) generally used these instruments:

Strings	Woodwind	Brass	Keyboard	Percussion
Violin I (6)	Flute (2)	2 Horns (2)	(none)	Timpani (2)
Violin 2 (6)	Oboe (2)	2 Trumpets (2)		
Viola (4)	Clarinets (2)			
Cello (3)	Bassoon (2)			
Bass (2)				

Teaching Music Across History

The Romantic orchestra (1825–1900) generally used these instruments:

Strings	Woodwind	Brass	Keyboard	Percussion
Violin I (16)	Piccolo (1)	Horns (4)	Piano (1)	Timpani (1)
Violin 2 (16)	Flute (3)	Trumpets (4)	Celesta (1)	Snare Drum (1)
Viola (12)	Oboe (3)	Trombones (4)	Organ (1)	Bass Drum (1)
Cello (10)	Clarinet (3)	Tuba (1)		Cymbals (1)
String Bass (8)	Bass Clarinet (1)			Triangle (1)
Harp (2)	English Horn (1)			Tambourine (1)
	Bassoon (2)			Glockenspiel (1)
				Xylophone (1)
				Chimes (1)

The Modern orchestra (1900–present) generally uses these instruments:

Strings	Woodwind	Brass	Keyboard	Percussion
Violin I (16)	Piccolo (1)	Horns (4)	Piano (1)	Timpani (1)
Violin 2 (14)	Flute (2)	Trumpets (3)	Celesta (1)	Snare Drum (1)
Viola (12)	Oboe (2)	Trombones (3)	Organ (1)	Bass Drum (1)
Cello (10)	Clarinet (2)	Euphonium (1)		Cymbals (1)
String Bass (8)	Bass Clarinet (1)	Tuba (1)		Triangle (1)
Harp (1)	Saxophone (1)			Tambourine (1)
	English Horn (1)			Glockenspiel (1)
	Bassoon (2)			Xylophone (1)
				Chimes (1)
				Vibraphone (1)
				Marimba (1)

Crack the Code

J.P. Money loved listening to the orchestras from each musical time period. He used the changes in the orchestra to create the code for his safe. If you organize the equations below, you will discover his secret code and unlock the safe for your school. Please add and subtract carefully—your school NEEDS that money!

1. How many total string players are in a Baroque orchestra? _____
   (Turn the dial to the right to this number.)

2. How many total string players are in a Modern orchestra? _____
   (Turn the dial to the left to this number.)

3. How many woodwind players are in the Classical orchestra? _____
   (Turn the dial to the right to this number.)

4. How many more woodwind players were added to the Romantic orchestra?

   _____ (Turn the dial to the right to this number.)

5. How many more total instruments were in the Romantic than the Baroque orchestra?

   _____ (Turn the dial to the left to this number, and open the safe.)

Cut here

– –

31

Arcangelo Corelli
Treasurer

Baroque Bucks

31

35 — Wolfgang A. Mozart, Treasurer — CLASSICAL CASH

103 — Edvard Grieg, Treasurer — ROMANTIC RICHES

99 — Aaron Copland, Treasurer — Modern Moo-Lah

NATIONAL MUSIC STANDARDS 8 & 9

"Sail! Sail! Sail Your Boat!"

★ **A Unit on the Mayflower**

Time Needed:
Approximately 30 minutes

Objective:
Using the information in a song and a story sheet, the students will gain an understanding of the sailing of the Mayflower.

Resources Needed:
✂ Teacher and student worksheets
✂ Song sheet

Lesson:
1. Ask students to tell you everything they know (or think they know) about the Mayflower.
   - ♪ The Mayflower was a sailing vessel that left Plymouth, England in 1620, and arrived in Plymouth, Massachusetts in 1621.
   - ♪ The Mayflower transported 102 passengers. About half of these passengers were commonly known as pilgrims who were searching for religious freedom.
   - ♪ The journey took 66 days.
   - ♪ Before landing, the majority of the passengers got together to write the famous Mayflower Compact which would be the basis for their temporary government.
   - ♪ The ship had been a wine ship with a 180 ton burden.
2. Read through the rebus lyrics as a class.
3. Learn and sing the song.

Answer Key

Sail

Ocean blue

The Pilgrims

Dream

Captain

New Land

Teaching Music Across History

The Mayflower

Verse One

🚢🚢🚢 your boat, across the 🌊, 👪 had a special 👨(🚢), they would make come true.

Verse Two

🚢🚢🚢 your boat, across the 🌊, **102** passengers boarded the ship, with the 👮 and the crew.

Verse Three

🚢🚢🚢 your boat,

across the 🌅, **66** days to cross the sea,

before the land was in view.

Verse Four

🚢🚢🚢 your boat,

across the 🌅, from London to Cape Cod they went,

a 🏞️ to start anew.

Sail! Sail! Sail your Boat!

Lyrics by Valeaira Luppens

Sail! Sail! Sail your boat, A-cross the ocean blue. The Pil-grims had a spe-cial dream, that they would make come true.

Verse 2: Sail! Sail! Sail your boat!
         Across the ocean blue.
         One hundred two passengers boarded the craft,
         With the captain and the crew.

Verse 3: Sail! Sail! Sail your boat!
         Across the ocean blue.
         Sixty-six days to cross the sea,
         Before the land was in view.

Verse 4: Sail! Sail! Sail your boat!
         Across the ocean blue.
         From London to Cape Cod they went,
         A new land to start anew.

NATIONAL MUSIC STANDARDS 6 & 9

Peer Gynt Isn't Very Sweet!

Time Needed:
Approximately 30 minutes

Objective:
Students will identify the mood of selections from the Peer Gynt Suite, No. 1 and identify it as a nationalistic piece.

Resources Needed:
CD player/CD:
- ♪ *Peer Gynt Suite*: "In the Hall of the Mountain King"
- ♪ *Peer Gynt Suite*: "Ase's Death"
- ♪ *Peer Gynt Suite*: "Morning"
- ♪ *Peer Gynt Suite*: "Anitra's Dance"
- ✄ Student worksheet: *Peer Gynt Isn't Very Sweet!*
- ✄ Pencils

Lesson:
1. Pass out worksheets.
2. Explain to the students that they will hear excerpts from the *Peer Gynt Suite, No. 1*.
   - ♪ READ: A suite is an instrumental piece consisting of several shorter pieces. Some suites are taken from opera, ballets, or plays.
3. Edvard Grieg was a Norwegian composer who wrote music for a play titled *Peer Gynt*, based on a Norwegian fairy tale. There probably was a person named Peer Gynt at one time, but either way, folk tales (or made up stories) are passed down through generations, so everyone in Norway was familiar with these stories. The music for the play was turned into two different "suites," or smaller performance pieces.
   - ♪ The story is about a generally naughty Norwegian guy, named Peer Gynt. At the beginning of the story, he goes to a wedding and runs away with the bride, but immediately leaves her. Peer Gynt continues to have adventures and falls in love with the daughter of the Mountain King. The king decides Peer Gynt should stay in his kingdom and become a *troll*.
     - A. (Listen to all of "In the Hall of the Mountain King.") ***Describe the mood of the piece of music. (Answers will vary: spooky, scary, hurried, etc.)***
   - ♪ Peer Gynt returns home (to Norway) and finds his mother is dying. Listen to the sad music and imagine them pretending to ride in a sleigh together to heaven.
     - A. (Listen to the first **45 seconds** of "Ase's Death") ***Describe the mood of the piece of music. (Answers will vary: sad, slow)***

Teaching Music Across History

♪ After his mother's death, Peer travels the world, arriving in the desert.

   A. (Listen to the first **48 seconds** of "Morning") ***Describe the mood of the piece of music. (Answers will vary: gentle, bright, etc.)***

♪ While in the desert, Peer Gynt meets a beautiful dancing woman, named Anitra, and falls in love with her, but she'll have nothing to do with him and leaves.

   A. (Listen to the first 26 seconds of "Anitra's Dance") ***Describe the mood of the piece of music. (Answers will vary: After the opening chord, the music is lively and energetic.)***

4. Peer Gynt continues to have adventures in Egypt and finally returns home to Norway. The music of Peer Gynt is *"nationalistic"* because it was inspired by folk tales and folk music of the country of Norway. Many of the composers of the ***Romantic period*** (approximately 1810–1900) wrote *nationalistic* music.

Student Name: _____

Peer Gynt Isn't Very Sweet!

A "suite" (a homonym of "sweet") is an instrumental piece consisting of several shorter pieces. Some suites are taken from opera, ballets, or plays. Listen to the Norwegian folk story of **Peer Gynt** and answer the questions about the suite of music from the play.

Describe the mood of **"In the Hall of the Mountain King"** _____
_____

Describe the mood of **"Ase's Death"** _____
_____

Describe the mood of **"Morning"** _____
_____

Describe the mood of **"Anitra's Dance"** _____
_____

The music of Peer Gynt is *"nationalistic"* because it was inspired by folk tales and folk music of the country of Norway. Many of the composers of the 19th century wrote nationalistic music. Here are some words used to describe the music:

Accelerando (gradually getting faster)

Allegro (fast)

Bright

Crescendo (gradually getting louder)

Forte (loud volume)

Gentle

Graceful

Largo (slow)

Legato (smooth)

Minor (sad)

Piano (soft volume)

Presto (fast)

Scary

Spooky

Teaching Music Across History

NATIONAL MUSIC STANDARDS 1 & 9

Thanksgiving Trivia

★ **Singing a Thanksgiving Partner Song**

Time Needed:
Approximately 40 minutes

Objective:
Using the historical information relating to the first Thanksgiving as an anticipatory set, the students will learn and sing a Thanksgiving partner song.

Resources Needed:
- Student and teacher trivia question and answer sheets
- Pencils
- Song sheet

Lesson:
1. As an anticipatory set, ask the students to supply the answers from the Thanksgiving Trivia sheet.
2. Compare their answers with the answers found on the Thanksgiving trivia answer sheet.
3. Teach "Over the River and Through the Wood" to the class.
   - ♪ First, teach the original first verse and refrain of the song.
   - ♪ Second, teach the partner song.
   - ♪ Combine to create the harmony parts.
4. This song can also be performed using a larger ensemble for the original verse, and a smaller ensemble for the partner song.

Student Name: _____

Thanksgiving Trivia

Directions: Answer the following questions using complete sentences and correct punctuation.

1. When the pilgrims first arrived in America, they were ill-prepared to survive in the new land. Over half of them died after the first winter. Did an Indian named Tisquantum, later known as Squanto, from the Patuxet Tribe help teach the settlers how to survive?

   _____
   _____
   _____

2. Were all of the settlers at the 1621 harvest celebration immigrants who arrived on the Mayflower? _____

3. To eat, did the pilgrims use knives, forks, and spoons? _____
   _____

4. Was turkey served for the main course? _____
   _____

5. Did the pilgrims enjoy mashed potatoes, gravy, biscuits, and pumpkin pie? _____
   _____
   _____

6. For the feast the pilgrims were joined by 90 Native American Indians, who brought five deer to share. How long did the celebration last? _____
   _____
   _____

7. What games did the pilgrims and the Native American Indians enjoy playing?
   _____
   _____
   _____

8. Which president proclaimed Thanksgiving as a national holiday? _____
   _____
   _____

Answer to Thanksgiving Trivia

1. Yes. He gave them seeds to grow plants that would thrive in the area. He also taught them how to hunt and fish. He showed them how to tap the trees for maple sugar and how to gather berries.

2. Yes. Later others settlers arrived and joined the colonists.

3. They didn't use forks, but they did use knives, spoons, and their fingers. They also used cloth napkins to hold the hot meat so as not to burn their fingers. Large shells were used for serving spoons.

4. Probably not. Although turkeys were brought to the harvest, most historians believe that the main course consisted of deer, rabbits, geese, and ducks.

5. No. They most likely enjoyed clams, codfish, and eels from the ocean. The pilgrims had run out of flour so there were no pies or biscuits, but they enjoyed boiled pumpkin, peas, corn, squash, and beans. A favorite sweet treat was dried fruits and berries. They also enjoyed eating a corn pudding called nausamp.

6. The holiday lasted three days.

7. The pilgrims enjoyed playing a game similar to baseball called stoolball and the Wampanoags liked to take part in a strength pitching game to see who could throw a log the farthest.

8. President Abraham Lincoln proclaimed Thanksgiving as a national holiday on November 26, 1863.

Over the River and Through the Woods

Lydia Maria Child
Arr. by Valeaira Luppens

O-ver the ri-ver and through the wood to Grand-fa-ther's house we go! The horse knows the way to car-ry the sleigh through the white and drift-ed snow! O-ver the ri-ver and through the wood to Grand-fa-ther's house a-way! We

52 Teaching Music Across History

would not stop for doll or top, For this is Thanks-giv - ing Day!

Thanks-giv - ing Day! Thanks-giv - ing Day what a won-der-ful hol - i - day! There's

so much to eat and peo - ple to greet, and a ride in the one horse sleigh!

Teaching Music Across History

Thanks-giv-ing Day! Thanks-giv-ing Day! Pass the tur-key right a-way! The food is great, but I can't wait, to go out-side and play! Thanksgiv-ing day! Thanks-giv-ing Day what a won-der-ful hol-i day There's O-ver the ri-ver and through the wood to Grand-fa-ther's house we go! the

Teaching Music Across History

so much to eat and peo-ple to greet, and a ride in the one horse sleigh!

horse knows the way to car-ry the sleigh through the white and drift-ed snow!

Thanks-giv-ing Day! Thanks-giv-ing Day, pass the tur-key right a-way! The

O-ver the ri-ver and through the wood to Grand-fa-ther's house a-way! We

food is great, but I can't wait, to go out-side and play!

would not stop for doll or top, For this is Thanks-giv-ing Day!

Teaching Music Across History

NATIONAL MUSIC STANDARDS 8 & 9

Hansel and Gretel

Time Needed:
Approximately 40 minutes

Objective:
Using worksheets, an interactive computer site, and music from *Hansel and Gretel*, students will be exposed to the history of opera, as well as careers associated with this musical form.

Resources Needed:
- Computer with Internet access and speakers (or, if available, a computer lab)
- Projector
- Pencils
- Student sheets (Opera History and Job Application, which can be printed on the front and back of the same sheet)
- CD (*Hansel and Gretel* "Overture")

Lesson:
1. Pass out the first student sheet, Opera History.
2. Read aloud, taking turns. One idea is to play a popcorn reading game in which individual students read a passage (at least one sentence), and say "popcorn" and another student's name. Then the next student has to read a passage (at least one sentence).
   - Alternatively, the teacher can be the one in charge of saying "popcorn" and selecting the next student.
   - The teacher can also take a turn at reading to model fluency.
3. After reading the about the history of opera, discuss the following.
   - *Additional Info*: Hansel and Gretel was originally written in German, but has been translated into English
   - *Additional Info*: Hansel and Gretel is usually performed in December, since the first performance was in Germany on December 23. Note: the characters in the opera include an evil witch, easily highlighted in October if your December schedule is tight.
4. **TECHNOLOGY:** The non-profit Creative Kids Central hosts a website with the interactive feature "Hansel & Gretel: Design Your Own Opera" creativekidseducationfoundation.org/kids/opera/base.htm
   - If a portable laptop lab or computer lab is available, students will take turns performing tasks or work individually or in small groups.
5. Overview of Creative Kids Central Hansel and Gretel activities
   - OVERTURE (enter name for program credits/story synopsis)
   - Act 1 Scene 1 / DANCING IN THE COTTAGE (Costume Designer)
   - Act 1 Scene 2 / ANGRY MOTHER (Set Designer)
   - Act 1 Scene 3 / FATHER AND MOTHER (Properties Manager)
   - Act 1 Scene 4 / FRIGHTENED FATHER (Lighting Technician)

Teaching Music Across History

- ♪ Act 2 Scene 1 / LOST IN THE WOODS (Set Designer)
- ♪ Act 2 Scene 2 / ANGELS PRAYER (cursor includes interactive sparkle for magic)
- ♪ **INTERMISSION:**
    - A. BE A CONDUCTOR: Meet and conduct the orchestra.
        - Roll the mouse over the instruments to learn more about them.
        - Adjust balance (volume) with controls for each section (woodwind, brass, percussion, and strings).
    - B. BE A SET DESIGNER: Design your gingerbread house.
- ♪ Act 3 Scene 1 / GINGERBREAD HOUSE
- ♪ Act 3 Scene 2 / WITCH'S ENTRANCE (Technical Director)
- ♪ Act 3 Scene 3 / WITCH'S SPELL (Lighting Technician)
- ♪ Act 3 Scene 4 / WITCH'S SONG (Technical Director)
- ♪ Act 3 Scene 5 / WITCH AND HANSEL (Stage Direction/blocking)
- ♪ Act 3 Scene 6 / WITCH AND GRETEL (Lighting Technician)
- ♪ Act 3 Scene 7 / THE OVEN (Set Designer)
- ♪ Act 3 Scene 8 / HANSEL AND GRETEL CELEBRATE (Technical Effects Director)
- ♪ Act 3 Scene 9 / PARENTS FIND HANSEL AND GRETEL (Finale)
- ♪ FINAL BOWS (students may throw roses to the cast)
- ♪ Go Backstage
    - A. About the Composer
    - B. What Is an Opera
    - C. Opera Glossary
    - D. Fairy Tales
    - E. Voice Studio
    - F. Teacher Downloads: Lesson Plans, Libretto and Text, Puppet Activity, and "Fractured Fairytales" (changing the storyline).
- ♪ If students work as a whole group, you have the additional opportunity to discuss and answer questions about each career as it is introduced.

6. If they're not on the back of the Opera History sheets, pass out the Job Application worksheets.
7. Listen again to the "Overture" (CD). Students will reflect upon which operatic career they would most enjoy and why.
    - ♪ *Make it a real life experience by saying*: "Your local opera company will be presenting a new production of *Hansel and Gretel*. Your parents have asked me to help you find a job to pay for the holiday gifts you're giving to your family and friends. The application process is simple: listen again to the "Overture" from *Hansel and Gretel* and reflect upon which job *you* would be best at, and why. Be sure to capitalize the first letter, and use punctuation and correct spelling to impress your future boss." (*Answers will vary*)
8. Walk around the room and read student responses.
9. Select a variety of students to participate in a mock interview in front of the class, playing the CD softly in the background during the interview process.
10. Ask questions as you read their job application response for the class. Discuss the job requirements and hire them on the spot!

Opera History

The musical style of "opera" began in Italy during the end of the Renaissance period (late 1500s) by noblemen who were trying to recreate classic Greek plays. Greeks used music in their plays as far back as the 5th century B.C., so Italians added music and began to sing their lines. Soon after that, composers began writing music for original plays. The musical form of opera rapidly became popular all over Europe and allowed singers to show off their voices and emotions.

The word "opera" is the Italian word for "work," probably because of all the work involved putting together a show including an orchestra, many singers, dancers, costumes, and scenery! Operas were usually written in Italian, since Italians invented the style and the storyline. Many operas are taken from historical events, mythology, fairy tales, and folk stories. Often the opera begins with an ***"Overture,"*** which introduces the musical ideas so the listener will recognize them later in the story.

As opera began to develop in the Baroque period (approximately 1600–1725), it became very fancy. During the Classical period (approximately 1725–1827), a composer named Christoph Willibald Gluck decided it should represent "beautiful simplicity," so he wrote vocal melodies that were simple and increased the importance of the orchestra. During the Romantic period (approximately 1827–1900), composers began to write operas in many languages (German, French, English, Spanish, Russian, and Italian).

Modern opera productions require many talented and creative individuals.

Think about it: *What job could you do?*

Job Application

Please read the list of available jobs and select a job you would enjoy.

Singer/Performer: The singer's job requires strong singing and acting skills.

Costume Designer: The costume designer must have an understanding of history and costumes. They must also be able to work well with the stage director and set designer to create a professional-looking performance.

Set Designer: The set designer creates backdrops for the action of the story.

Properties Manager: The properties ("props") manager makes sure each performer has objects to help tell the story.

Lighting Technician: The lighting technician highlights soloists with spotlights and creates moods with lights on the stage.

Conductor: The conductor directs the musicians (singers and instrumentalists) so they stay in balance and together.

Technical (Effects) Director: Sometimes, special effects are required to tell a story. The technical effects director helps the actors with trap doors and "rigging" (a counterweight system) to create these special effects.

I'm applying for the job of: _____.

Why would you be good at this job? _____

_____

_____

_____

Applicant's (your) name: _____

NATIONAL MUSIC STANDARD 9

The Nutcracker

Time Needed:
Approximately 40 minutes

Objective:
The students will explore the history and story of *The Nutcracker* suite and ballet.

Resources Needed:
- Computer with Internet access and speakers (or, if available, a computer lab)
- Crayons
- Pencils
- CD (*Nutcracker Suite*)

Optional: the Nutcracker picture book from your school library
Optional: show video excerpts from the second act from web resources

Student sheets
- Tchaikovsky's biography
- Nutcracker coloring sheet
- Sugar Plum Fairy coloring sheet
- *Anchor activity* The Nutcracker Maze   **brb.org.uk/pdf/Maze1.pdf**

Additional Storybook Links

bbc.co.uk/cbeebies/christmas/stories/christmas-nutcracker/

Lesson:
1. Pass out Tchaikovsky's biography.
2. Read the biography.
3. **TECHNOLOGY:** Listen to the story of *The Nutcracker* found on the BBC website for younger listeners. (You can add the link to your web favorites or create a link on a blog or webpage for quick access.)
    - Optional: If you don't have access to technology, or just want to be able to discuss the text and storyline in greater detail, use *The Nutcracker* picture book from your school's library. There are many versions of the book and each of them can be an excellent resource to give students strong mental pictures and provide historical context.
4. Pass out the coloring sheets, allowing the students to choose one or both of the images to color (the Nutcracker or the Sugar Plum Fairy).
5. Play selections from *The Nutcracker* (CD) while students enjoy coloring the characters.
    - If some students finish early, give them the *anchor activity* Nutcracker maze. **brb.org.uk/pdf/Maze1.pdf**
    - Optional: show excerpts from the second act from web video resources.

Teaching Music Across History

Piotr Ilyich Tchaikovsky

Good day, my name is Piotr Tchaikovsky and I was born in Russia, on May 7, 1840. When I was 8 years old, my family moved to St. Petersburg, where my parents thought I should become a lawyer because being a musician wasn't an acceptable position.

I continued to study music in law school, and eventually, gave up law and went to the St. Petersburg Conservatory. After graduation, I moved to Moscow to teach music at a conservatory there, which is now called the Tchaikovsky Conservatory…I think it has a nice ring to it!

Nadezhda von Meck, a wealthy widow, helped to support me financially. We never met, but I wanted to repay her kindness, so I dedicated my fourth symphony to her.

Before *The Nutcracker* ballet was performed in 1892, I selected eight of the dances to be performed as *The Nutcracker Suite*. A suite is an instrumental piece consisting of several shorter pieces. Some suites are taken from opera and ballets, like *The Nutcracker*. *The Nutcracker Suite* was originally more popular than the ballet. In fact, I didn't really care for the music at first, but it grew on me. I hope it grows on you, too!

Student Name: _____

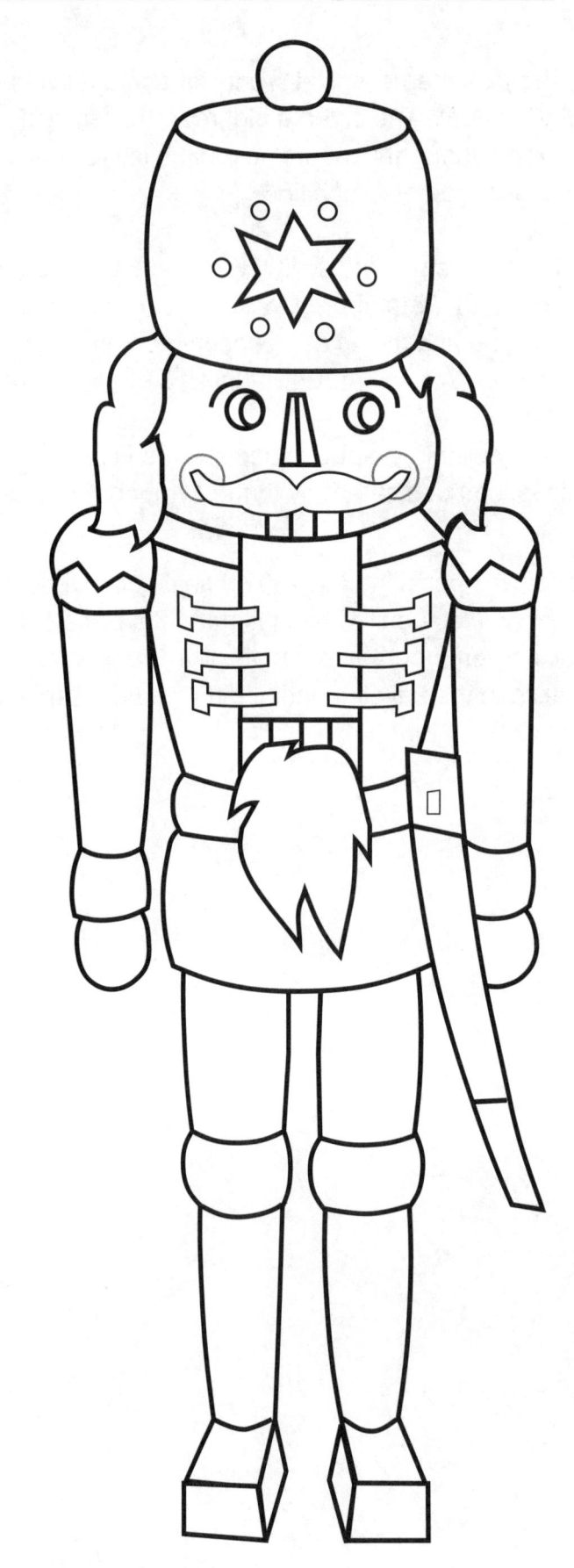

62 Teaching Music Across History

Student Name: _____

Teaching Music Across History

NATIONAL MUSIC STANDARDS 1 & 9

Martin Luther King, Jr.

★ **Brief Overview of Martin Luther King., Jr.**

Time Needed:
Approximately 30 to 40 minutes

Objective:
The students will gain a better understanding of the life of Martin Luther King, Jr. by using the clues given in the student sheets and learning a song that reflects the viewpoints he wished to impart.

Resources Needed:
✂ Student sheets
✂ Song sheets

Lesson:
1. As an anticipatory set, explain to the students that you will be reading some of the events from a famous person's life. Challenge them to see who can correctly identify the individual first.

2. After the class discovers who the person is, distribute the "Who Am I?" sheets to the students and finish reading the descriptive clues together.

3. Teach and sing the *Martin Luther King, Jr.* song.

Teaching Music Across History

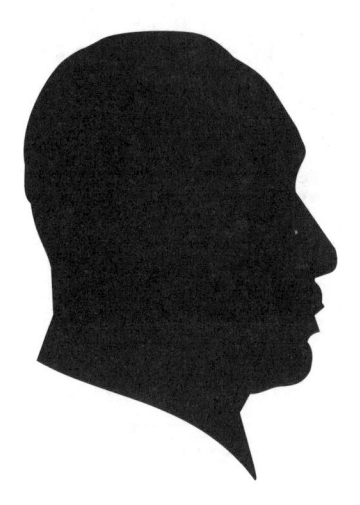

Who Am I?

1. I was born on January 15, 1929.

2. I was a middle child. I had an older sister and a younger brother.

3. I had my first name changed from Michael to Martin.

4. I graduated from high school at the age of 15.

5. I married a beautiful woman named Coretta Scott in 1953, and we had four children.

6. I earned my doctorate degree in 1955.

7. My grandfather was a minister, my father was a minister, and I became a minister.

8. From 1957 to 1968, I devoted my life to improving civil rights. I thought it was unfair that people were treated differently based on the color of their skin or their beliefs. I wrote five books and travelled the world speaking to others, urging them to end the injustices that existed.

9. One of my most famous speeches was called "I Have a Dream."

10. At the age of 35, I was the youngest man to receive the Nobel Peace Prize.

11. President Lyndon Johnson agreed with my beliefs and signed the Civil Rights Act in 1964, which gave every American equal rights. In 1965, the Voting Rights Bill was passed, assuring every adult American had the right to vote.

12. The changes made to treat everyone fairly were welcomed by most, but some disagreed adamantly. Unfortunately I made some enemies on my quest for equality. I was assassinated by one of these men on April 4, 1968.

13. I was only 39 years old when I died, but I helped change the course of my people before my untimely death.

14. Today there is a national holiday that celebrates my life on the third Monday in January.

Martin Luther King Jr.

Destiny Roberts and Valeaira Luppens

Ev-ery sin-gle day, He fought for what was right. Fair-ness for one and all, Not just for the whites! He knew that we should not be judged on the co-lor of our skin.

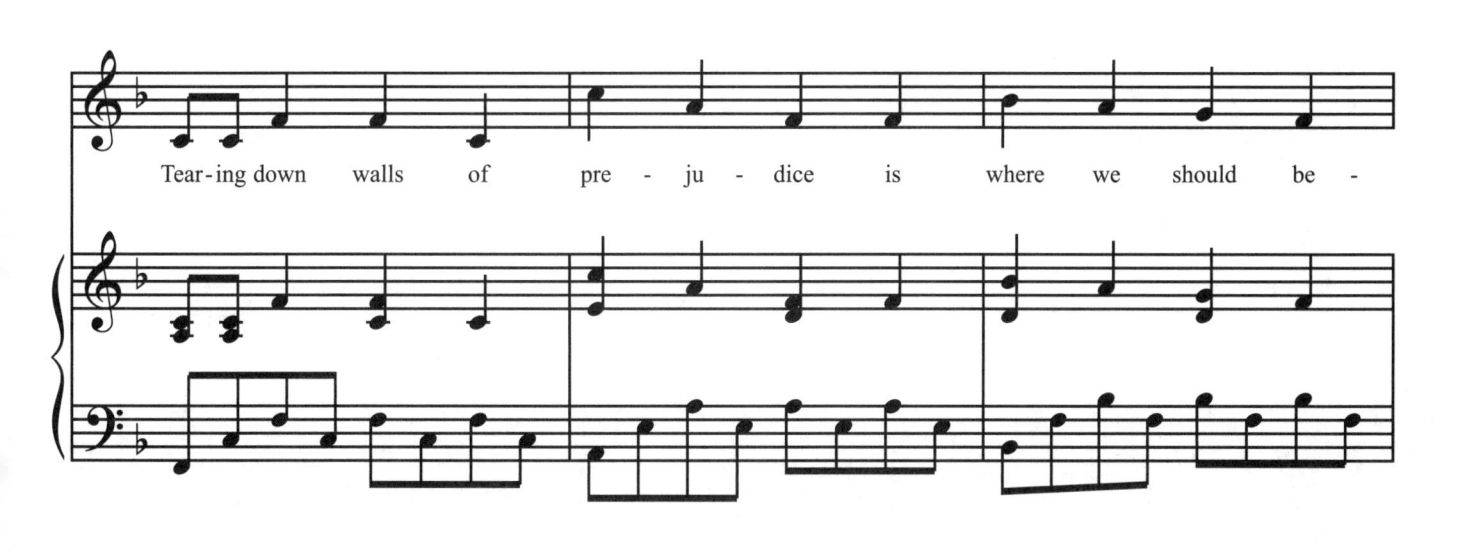

Tear-ing down walls of pre-ju-dice is where we should be-gin! He was just a man, but he

had a spe - cial dream. Preach - ing e - qua - li -
ty, was his fo - cal theme. E - ven
though he was a peace - ful man, He died a vio - lent

death, He knew he'd made pro-gress as he drew his fi-nal breath!

Teaching Music Across History

NATIONAL MUSIC STANDARD 9

Chit Chat

Time Needed:
Approximately 30 minutes

Objective:
Students will create dialogue between three historic characters while listening to *Tritsch Tratsch Polka* (*Chit Chat Polka*).

Resources Needed:
- CD (*Tritsch Tratsch Polka*) and CD player
- Student sheets
- Pencils

Lesson:
1. Listen to *Tritsch Tratsch Polka* and tell students that "tritsch tratsch" means "chit chat," or conversation.
2. Pass out the student sheets.
3. Read, as a group, the three biographies (George Washington Gale Ferris, Walter Camp, and Oscar Mayer).
    - Popcorn reading: Read the first paragraph and stop abruptly, having the entire class say the next missing word. (This helps keep students' attention on the text).
    - Take turns reading each paragraph, allowing students to be the readers. (This will give weaker readers the chance to stop on difficult words, while the entire class fills in the blank.)
    - Discuss each paragraph:
        A. Have you ever ridden on a Ferris wheel?
        B. How are football uniforms different from Camp's time? (More protective gear: helmets, shoulder pads, etc.)
        C. Have you ever eaten any Oscar Mayer products?
4. Play the music *Tritsch Tratsch Polka* while students create chit chat between the characters.
    - Ferris's dialogue is completed to give an example of expectations.
5. Read selected dialogue aloud with the music.
    - Answers will vary.

70 Teaching Music Across History

Johann Strauss, Jr. was born in 1825, in Vienna. His father was a very famous musician, but was against his son following in his career. Johann Jr. ignored his father's advice and started an orchestra when he was 19 years old. He traveled a great deal with his orchestra and, while in Russia, got the idea for *Tritsch Tratsch Polka* when he was 34 years old. "Tritsch tratsch" may be translated as "chit chat" (and was also the name of Mrs. Strauss's poodle).

These three historical figures were all born in **1859**, the same year Johann Strauss, Jr. wrote the **Tritsch Tratsch Polka**.

George Washington Gale Ferris, inventor of the Ferris wheel, attended an engineer's banquet in 1891 hosted by the planners of the Chicago World's Fair of 1893. They were asked to plan a structure that would be better than the Eiffel Tower, which was the star of Paris's International Exposition of 1889. His inspiration came from an undershot water wheel he had seen as a small boy on the Carson River. Ferris's structure elevated the riders 26 stories in the air for about 10 minutes, carrying them around two times. The wheel cost $250,000 to construct, but being the most popular attraction at the Chicago World's Fair, it made almost $750,000.

Walter Camp, the "Father of American football," attended Yale from 1876 to 1882, studying medicine and business. He eventually became general athletic director and head advisory football coach at Yale University from 1888–1914, and chairman of the Yale football committee from 1888–1912. Among his many innovations, Camp is recognized for adding the snap-back from center, the system of downs, cutting the number of players from 15 to 11, and measuring the lines on the field. His changes to the traditional rugby game helped make the American version of college football become very popular!

Oscar Mayer, a butcher in Chicago, was a German immigrant who built a two-story building for his business and family. As the company grew, he sponsored polka bands and the Chicago World's Fair of 1893. In 1936, Oscar's nephew designed the Wienermobile, a hot dog and bun shaped automobile. As the brand became more famous, Oscar Mayer opened factories in Davenport, Iowa; Los Angeles; Milwaukee; and Philadelphia. He eventually employed over 9,000 workers. The company was later sold to General Foods and now is known as Kraft.

Teaching Music Across History

Student Name: _____

Directions: "Tritsch tratsch" means "chit chat," or a casual conversation. After you've read all three biographies, write a brief conversation you imagine the men could have had while listening to Tritsch Tratsch Polka.

If these three gentlemen met, what do you suppose they would chit chat about?

George Washington Gale Ferris would say, "Hi, my name is George Ferris. Have you ever ridden a 'Ferris Wheel?' I invented it for the Chicago World's Fair!"

Walter Camp would say, _____

_____

_____

Oscar Mayer would say, _____

_____

_____

If you met them, what would you chit chat about? _____

_____

_____

_____

_____

72 Teaching Music Across History

NATIONAL MUSIC STANDARD 9

Favorite Songs

★ **Examining the Components That Create a Favorite Song**

Time Needed:
30 minutes

Objective:
The students will understand the roles of melody, rhythm, and lyrics in popular music.

Resources Needed:
- Recording of teacher's favorite song
- Computer with Internet access and speakers (or, if available, a computer lab)
- Online video of "Dixie"
- Online video of "Balm in Gilead"
- Student worksheets
- Pencils
- Small slips of paper for survey

Lesson:
1. Listen to the teacher's favorite song. (Select a song with appeal to your student population to increase their interest in the lesson.)
2. Ask the students to analyze the exact reasons the teacher chose this particular song as his/her personal favorite. (Answers will vary.)
3. Distribute student worksheets and pencils.
4. As a class, read through the brief description of a great song.
5. Read the description of Lincoln's favorite song, listen to a performance of the song, then instruct students to determine which of the three components most influenced the president's choice in his selection of this song. (They can select more than one, but must give a reason why they chose that specific answer.)
6. Follow suit with Martin Luther King, Jr.'s favorite song.
7. Next, ask the students to write down the name of their favorite song on a small slip of paper. (This process will help eliminate peer pressure and help validate the honesty of the survey.) Remind the students that songs should be school appropriate.
8. List all the songs on the board and tally them as you go.
9. Analyze the three components of the song that won, and determine which of the three elements contributed to the success of the song.

What Makes a Song Great?

A simplified answer to this question can be narrowed down to three components:

- ♪ **Melody** – Does the song have a catchy tune that keeps you singing it over and over?
- ♪ **Rhythm** – Does the rhythm of the song move you?
- ♪ **Lyrics** – Are the words in this song especially meaningful to you? Does it remind you of a special person, place, or event in your life?

Below are two examples of a favorite song enjoyed by a well-known person. After reading a brief description of the song, decide which element you think led to their choice. (In some cases you may decide to select more than one of the components.) Give a specific reason for your selection.

Abraham Lincoln, the 16th President of the United States, reportedly enjoyed a wide variety of music ranging from the opera to the popular music of his time. He was once quoted saying, "I have always thought 'Dixie' one of the best tunes I have ever heard." The lyrics of the first verse are as follows:

> I wish I was in the land of cotton,
>
> Old times they are not forgotten;
>
> Look away! Look away! Look away! Dixie Land.
>
> In Dixie Land where I was born,
>
> Early on one frosty mornin',
>
> Look away! Look away! Look away! Dixie Land.

Which characteristic(s) made this song so special to Abraham Lincoln?

1. Melody: _____

_____

2. Rhythm: _____

_____

3. Lyrics: _____

_____

Teaching Music Across History

Martin Luther King, Jr. was a Baptist minister who promoted the Civil Rights Movement for African Americans. He wanted to end racial segregation and discrimination and received the Nobel Peace Prize for his efforts to help achieve this goal. After his death, he also received the Congressional Gold Medal and is honored every year on Martin Luther King, Jr. Day. King had several favorite songs, but his wife claimed that he liked listening to "Balm in Gilead" when he needed inspiration. The lyrics of the first verse and chorus are:

There is a balm in Gilead	Sometimes I feel discouraged,
To make the wounded whole;	And think my work's in vain,
There is a balm in Gilead	But then the Holy Spirit
To heal the sin-sick soul.	Revives my soul again.

Which characteristic(s) made this song so special to Martin Luther King, Jr.?

1. Melody: _____

_____

2. Rhythm: _____

_____

3. Lyrics: _____

_____

My current favorite song is:

_____

Which characteristic(s) make this song so special to me?

1. Melody: _____

_____

2. Rhythm: _____

_____

3. Lyrics: _____

_____

Teaching Music Across History

NATIONAL MUSIC STANDARD 9

George Washington

Time Needed:
Approximately 30 minutes

Objective:
Using both the biography and rap sheet of George Washington, the students will develop a basic overview of our first president's life.

Resources Needed:
- Student biography sheet
- Student rap sheet
- Rap accompaniment music (optional)

Lesson:
1. As an anticipatory set, ask the students to identify the name of the first president of the United States.

2. Next, encourage the students to list the facts they know about Washington's life and write them on the board.

3. After reviewing the words on the rebus key, explain that the teacher will read the biography except for the rebus words which the students will interject.

4. After they've heard George Washington's biography and contributed the rebus words, ask the students to add more facts to the board.

5. Teach and perform the George Washington rap.

   ♪ If the students are very young, the teacher can read the first two lines of the rap while the students read and clap the last two lines.

George Washington's Biography

Rebus Key:

| George | Born | 16 | Married | Happy | Constitution |

[George] was [born] in 1732, on a quiet Virginia plantation. His parents raised him to be a Southern gentleman who was both intelligent and mannerly. When [George] was [16], he became a surveyor and explored the lands in Shenandoah. A few years later, he fought in a few minor conflicts which led to the French and Indian War.

[George] [married] Martha Dandridge Custis. He loved overseeing his lands where he lived in Mount Vernon. He also served in the Virginia House of Burgesses. Most of the time, he was very [happy], except when he had to follow the strict rules the British had required the colonists to keep. In 1775, [George] became the Commander in Chief of the Continental Army and faithfully led his troops for six long years during the Revolutionary War. In 1781, the British finally surrendered and the war was over.

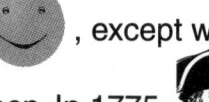

[George] attended the Constitutional Convention in Philadelphia that resulted in the writing of the [Constitution]. When the [Constitution] was approved, [George] was elected as the first President of the United States of America, and took office on April 30, 1789. [George] served two terms, then retired to his beloved Mount Vernon. He is known today as the "Father of Our Country."

Teaching Music Across History

Georgie's Rap

Hup! Two! Three! Four!
Who's that knockin' at our door?
It's Georgie! (Clap! Clap! Clap!)
It's Georgie! (Clap! Clap! Clap!)

Born in 1732,
Virginia's land is where he grew!
It's Georgie! (Clap! Clap! Clap!)
It's Georgie! (Clap! Clap! Clap!)

Commander of the army,
To help set our country free!
It's Georgie! (Clap! Clap! Clap!)
It's Georgie! (Clap! Clap! Clap!)

He attended the convention,
Where our constitution was written!
It's Georgie! (Clap! Clap! Clap!)
It's Georgie! (Clap! Clap! Clap!)

He was our very first president,
Voted by unanimous consent.
It's Georgie! (Clap! Clap! Clap!)
It's Georgie! (Clap! Clap! Clap!)

The Father of our great country,
He goes down in history!
It's Georgie! (Clap! Clap! Clap!)
It's Georgie! (Clap! Clap! Clap!)

NATIONAL MUSIC STANDARDS 2 & 9

A Lincoln Portrait

Time Needed:
Approximately 30 minutes

Objective:
Students will chorally read an excerpt of *A Lincoln Portrait*, by Aaron Copland

Resources Needed:
- Computer with Internet access and speakers (or, if available, a computer lab)
- *A Lincoln Portrait* (excerpt): CD
- Student scripts

Lesson:
1. Discuss the following information with the students.

   A. Lincoln's Gettysburg Address gave closing remarks for the dedication of the Gettysburg soldier's cemetery. The main speaker was **Edward Everett**, whose speech was very long and boring, so the crowd became fidgety.

   B. Lincoln said, *"the world will little note, nor long remember what we say here."* On the contrary, his speech was meaningful, short, and very powerful.

      1. Lincoln had thought about the content of this speech for a long period of time and was a fiery speaker.
      2. The Gettysburg Address has become a very popular speech.

   C. There is a popular myth that President Lincoln scribbled the Gettysburg Address on the back of an envelope. *This isn't true*. The rough draft was written on White House stationery prior to the trip, and he revised the speech when he arrived at Gettysburg, Pennsylvania.

2. *TECHNOLOGY:* Watch the entire Gettysburg Address, animated by Adam Gault, and listen to the speaker's meaningful tone: http://vimeo.com/15402603

3. Pass out student sheets and play the excerpt of "A Lincoln Portrait," listening for the expression of the narrator.

4. Practice reading the script and perform it along with the recording.
   - The script can be rehearsed/memorized over the period of several classes.
   - The choral reading can be performed at an assembly around Presidents' Day or as part of a February Black History Month activity.

5. Discuss the narration's main idea (answers may vary). *Lincoln thought that democracy shouldn't support slavery and our government had the opportunity for rebirth, ensuring our system of democracy would be strengthened and continue for generations.*

6. Enrichment (to supplement this lesson you may utilize the following options):

   A. *TECHNOLOGY*: Lincoln Memorial: http://www.nps.gov/linc/index.htm
   - Lincoln Memorial virtual tour (Gettysburg Address on left wall)
   - Lincoln Memorial flipbook (requires FlashPlayer)

   B. *TECHNOLOGY:* Interactive Gettysburg Address by the Smithsonian Museum: americanhistory.si.edu/documentsgallery/exhibitions/gettysburg_address_1.html

Student Name: _____

A Lincoln Portrait, (excerpt) by Aaron Copland

"Lincoln was a quiet man. Abe Lincoln was a quiet and a melancholy man. But when he spoke of democracy, this is what he said.

"He said: 'As I would not be a slave, so I would not be a master. This expresses my idea of democracy. Whatever differs from this, to the extent of the difference, is no democracy.

"Abraham Lincoln, 16th president of these United States, is everlasting in the memory of his countrymen. For on the battleground at Gettysburg, this is what he said.

"He said: 'That from these honored dead we take increased devotion to that cause for which they gave the last full measure of devotion. That we here highly resolve that these dead shall not have died in vain. That this nation under God shall have a new birth of freedom and that government of the people, by the people, and for the people shall not perish from the earth.'"

What is the narration's main idea?

_____

_____

_____

_____

_____

NATIONAL MUSIC STANDARD 9

Election Day

Time Needed:
Approximately 30 minutes

Objective:
Students will explore the process of voting, including the presidential election and a mock "lifetime achievement" film composer award.

Resources Needed:
- Student sheets
- Pencils

Lesson:
1. As an anticipatory set, ask the students, "Who is the current president of the United States?"
2. Pass out the Election Day student sheets.
3. Read the requirements for voting in a presidential election.
4. Ask the students, "Has anyone ever watched an awards show like the Grammys or the Academy Awards?"
5. Discuss how these awards recognize great work in the fields of music and film.
6. Read the biographies and film score works for John Williams and Daniel Robert Elfman.
7. Encourage students to add a write-in vote if they have another favorite film composer. Don't forget about pop musicians who have created music for films, such as Michael Jackson, whose music was featured in the film *"This Is It."*

Election Day

An election day is a day set aside for people to cast their votes for a candidate they would like to represent them. Election days occur across the world, but in the United States, the official date is the Tuesday after the first Monday in November during even-numbered years. Presidential elections are held every four years. At the elections, we select candidates who we hope will represent our beliefs and well-being and keep our government strong.

Elections are held at a polling place close to where the voter lives. Their votes are recorded on ballots and then tabulated to determine who wins.

Election Day is important because it helps preserve our democracy. In order to vote, the person must be:

1. Eighteen years old or older
2. A registered voter
3. A United States citizen
4. Voters must live in the same state they vote in

All Americans have not always had the right to vote. Each state had its own regulations. Often, only white men who owned land had the privilege of voting. In the mid-1800s, white men who did not own land were allowed to vote. Then in 1870, when the 15th Amendment to the Constitution was added, all men were allowed to vote. When the 19th Amendment was added 50 years later, women were allowed to vote, too. Finally, in 1924, The Indian Citizenship Act was created so that Native Americans could vote.

Here are some candidates of another kind:

John Williams

John Towner Williams was born in New York on February 8, 1932. His father was a jazz percussionist who played with a quintet. John became an outstanding composer, pianist, and conductor. Over the course of his career he wrote some of the most famous film scores ever, including the music for **Star Wars, Jaws, Superman, Indiana Jones, E.T., Hook, Jurassic Park, Home Alone,** and three of the **Harry Potter** films. He has received a host of awards for his impact in the music world, ranging from five Academy Awards and four Golden Globe Awards to numerous Grammy Awards!

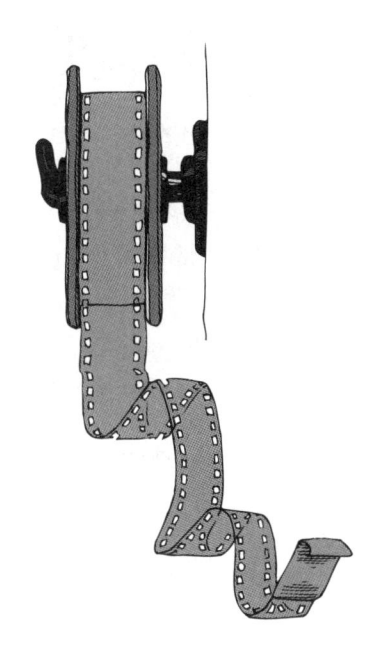

Danny Elfman

Daniel Robert Elfman was born in Los Angeles, California on May 29, 1953. Danny has composed many songs and scores for movies, including the music for **Men in Black I, II, and III; Pee-wee's Big Adventure**; **Edward Scissorhands**; **Batman Returns; Black Beauty; Mission: Impossible; Spy Kids; Charlie and the Chocolate Factory;** and **Alice in Wonderland.**

The Academy is presenting a special "Lifetime Achievement" award to a great film composer. We need you to vote for your favorite movie composer to represent what you feel makes great film music.

Nominee:	Vote here:
• John Towner Williams	
• Daniel Robert "Danny" Elfman	
• Write-in candidate:	

Teaching Music Across History

NATIONAL MUSIC STANDARD 9

Let My People Go!

Time Needed:
Approximately 30 minutes

Objective:
Students will take a virtual trip on the underground railroad while listening to music reflecting the culture of the time period.

Resources Needed:
- Computer with Internet access and speakers (or, if available, a computer lab)
- Pencils
- Student worksheet

Lesson:
1. Discuss what students know about the "Underground Railroad," the system of secret paths and safe houses used by slaves to escape to free states and Canada. This was done with the help of former slaves like Harriet Tubman, and "abolitionists"—people who wanted to abolish slavery.

2. TECHNOLOGY: Access the virtual Underground Railroad trip at nationalgeographic.com/railroad/. This can be projected on a screen or an interactive whiteboard for whole group instruction or students can take the virtual tour individually in a computer lab.

   - Enter the Underground Railroad.
   - Choose: Yes, I want to go!
   - Moses is coming! Follow Harriet Tubman.
   - "Steal Away" (African American spiritual)
   - Fearful choices: Yes, I'll approach the house.
   - Safe station
   - Strange new world
   - Breathing free
   - Near the border
   - Frightening frontier: Yes, only Canada is truly safe.
   - The promised land: Free at last!

3. Look at the lyrics from "Go Down, Moses."
   - Spirituals were often used to keep the hope of freedom alive. Ask, "What do you think another meaning of these words could be?"

   A. Egypt's land: **_The South (plantations)_**

   B. Moses: **_Harriet Tubman (and others from the underground railroad)_**

   C. Pharaoh: **_Slave owners_**

   D. Canaan: **_Canada_**

   E. Bondage flee: **_Escape by the Underground Railroad_**

4. After looking at the lyrics, listen to various interpretations of the spiritual, including an online version by singer Paul Robeson, located at http://authentichistory.com/1600-1859/3-spirituals/1965_Go_Down_Moses-Paul_Robeson.html.

Teaching Music Across History

Student Name: _____

Look at the lyrics from **"Go Down, Moses."** Spirituals were often used to keep the hope of freedom alive. What do you think another meaning of these words could be?

When Israel was in Egypt's land,

Let my people go;

Oppressed so hard they could not stand,

Let my people go.

Refrain:

Go down, (go down) Moses, (Moses)

Way down in Egypt's land;

Tell old Pharaoh

To let my people go!

This world's a wilderness of woe,

Let my people go;

O let us on to Canaan go,

Let my people go.

(Refrain)

O let us all from bondage flee,

Let my people go;

And let us all in Christ be free,

Let my people go.

(Refrain)

Write your translation of what these words could have meant to the slaves below:

Egypt's land: _____

Moses: _____

Pharaoh: _____

Canaan: _____

Bondage flee: _____

Teaching Music Across History

NATIONAL MUSIC STANDARD 9

Bach's Court Trial

✶ **Brief Historic Overview of the Early Period of Bach**

Time Needed:
Approximately two class periods

Objective:
The students will gain an understanding of both courtroom procedure and Bach's struggle to maintain his integrity as a composer in his fight for musical freedom.

Resources Needed:
- Student worksheets
- Plain notepaper
- Pencils for note taking
- Teacher's choice of Bach music for a listening example

Free internet resource: last.fm/listen/artist/Johann Sebastian Bach/

Optional film: Bach's Fight for Freedom: imdb.com/title/tt0123396/

Lesson:
1. Have the students listen to a brief excerpt of your choice of Bach music while you give background information and distribute student supplies.
2. Explain that Bach was employed by Duke Wilhelm August of Weimar, but wanted to quit his job because he was offered a better job with Prince Leopold von Anhalt-Köthen. When he tried to leave, Duke Wilhelm August of Weimar put Bach in jail.
3. Explain to the students that they will be conducting a court case in the classroom, based on Johann Sebastian Bach's brief imprisonment in 1717.
4. Assign students to cover the following positions:
    - Judge
    - Bailiff
    - Prosecuting attorney (and assistants)
    - Defendant's attorney (and assistants)
    - Twelve Jurors
        A. If you wish to involve more students, you could either increase the size of the jury, or have two separate juries.
        B. It would be interesting to have each group discuss their decision at the end of the trial.
        C. The students should select someone to be the jury foreman.
    - First witness, Duke Wilhelm August of Weimar
    - Second witness, Maria Barbara
    - Third witness, Prince Leopold von Anhalt-Köthen
    - Fourth witness, Johann Sebastian Bach

5. Before the actual trial takes place, instruct the students to take notes relating to Bach's background:
   - Bach was born in Eisenach, Germany on March 21, 1685.
   - His family was well-known for being musicians.
   - His parents died when he was young and he was raised by his brother.
   - He learned to play both the organ and the violin.
   - At the age of 15, he became a boy soprano at Lüneberg, Germany.
   - During his teens, he began composing church music.
   - In 1703, Bach became the organist at Arnstadt, Germany.
   - At the age of 22, he moved and became the organist at Mühlhausen, Germany. He focused on writing church music at this time because he was very religious.
   - Bach married his cousin, Maria Barbara.
   - Bach was a very religious man. Because of dissension within the Lutheran church, he decided to move to Weimar, Germany where he could focus on his own beliefs and compose the type of music he wished to write.

6. Finally, hand a copy of the court notes to each of the witnesses and both attorneys (and their assistants) to study. They will base their questions (which should be written down) and responses on the information on the sheets. Encourage the students to be creative and try to build a solid case.
   - *Optional*: Set up your classroom to resemble a courtroom. If possible, the judge should wear a black choir robe and have a gavel. Place the judge at the teacher's desk with the witness chair placed next to him/her. The jury would be seated at the side of the room.

7. Conduct the trial, following the script.

8. After the jury's verdict, discuss the outcome of the trial.

9. *Written question*: Do you believe Johann Sebastian Bach should remain as the employee of Duke Wilhelm August of Weimar or should he be allowed to become the employee of Prince Leopold von Anhalt-Köthen? Why? *(Answers will vary.)*

10. Optional film: *Bach's Fight for Freedom*.

Background Notes for Court Case

Duke Wilhelm August of Weimar

1. I commissioned Bach to be the court organist at Weimar in 1708.
2. Bach worked as both an organist and as the Konzertmeister (concert master) in Weimar.
3. Once he started becoming famous, he became more demanding. When he didn't get offered the position of Kapellmeister, he decided to leave.
4. When Bach refused to compose after being offered a post with the prince, I felt that Bach was rejecting the beliefs of his church.
5. I also felt that Bach should have remained loyal out of respect for his superiors. I have supported Bach and his family for the past nine years and don't like the way he asked to resign from his position, so I had him imprisoned.

Maria Barbara

1. I married Bach after he received his job at Mühlhausen, Germany in October 1707.
2. Johann and I are very happily married.
3. We had six beautiful and talented children together. Sadly, three died at a very early age. (A seventh child would be born a year later in 1718.)
4. I strongly believe that my husband is a very dedicated family man and a deeply religious man. By moving, our children will be able to go to a better school and my husband will happier. He and the prince get along very well.
5. We should be allowed to live wherever we choose. We are not indentured servants.

Prince Leopold von Anhalt-Köthen

1. My sister married the nephew of Bach's Weimar employer. She met Bach in Weimar and thought he was wonderful. When offered the position of Kapellmeister, Bach eagerly accepted.
2. I enjoy playing the viola da gamba, and wanted Bach to conduct the court orchestra.
3. I respected Bach and his musical genius and felt that Bach respected me as well.
4. I believed the only reason the Duke didn't want Bach to leave was because of a petty past rivalry.
5. I feel that Bach should be allowed to work wherever he chooses.

Johann Sebastian Bach

1. I moved to Weimar for nine years. During the first six years, I was the church organist. During the last three years, I was promoted and became the Konzertmeister (conductor) of the court orchestra.
2. My fame began to spread during this period as both a composer and a performer. Not only was I writing works for the organ, I was also writing cantatas for the court chapel.
3. I became upset when I should have been offered, but wasn't, the position of Kapellmeister after Johann Samuel Drese passed away. So I started looking for a better position elsewhere.
4. Within months, I was offered a position by Prince Leopold von Anhalt-Köthen.
5. I informed my employer of my intent to leave and was thrown into jail.
6. I believe I have the right to be happy and should be allowed to work where I choose. I am not an indentured slave.

Students' Statement: "I can connect with historical events."

Courtroom Procedure

Jury is seated.

Bailiff: All rise and give your attention. The Court of Weimar, Germany is now in session. Honorable Judge _____ will be presiding today.

(Everyone stands as the judge walks in. After the judge is seated, everyone else may be seated.)

Judge: The first case on the docket today will be the suit that has been filed by Duke Wilhelm August of Weimar against Johann Sebastian Bach. Are the counsels ready to give their opening statements?

Prosecutor and **Defendant Attorney:** We are, Your Honor.

Judge: Then let the proceeding begin.

Prosecutor's opening statement: *Summarizes the evidence he/she has against Bach and explains why Bach should remain in jail until he agrees to comply with Duke Wilhelm August of Weimar's terms.*

Defendant Attorney's opening statement: *Explains that Johann Sebastian Bach has every right to seek employment elsewhere. He will prove that Bach is simply pursuing better living conditions for his family while trying to seek employment in an environment that offers him more opportunities to develop his music.*

Judge: It is now time for the prosecutor to build his/her case.

Prosecution calls First Witness: Duke Wilhelm August of Weimar

Defense: *Cross examines, or tries to break down any evidence the prosecution has against Bach.*

Defense begins his/her case.

Defense calls First Witness: Maria Barbara Bach. *Defense should interview the witness, asking her why she feels Bach should be allowed to leave the court of Duke Wilhelm August of Weimar.*

Prosecution: *Cross examines.*

Defense calls Second Witness: Prince Leopold. *Defense should interview the witness, asking him why he feels Bach should be allowed to leave the court of Duke Wilhelm August of Weimar.*

Prosecution: *Cross examines.*

Defense calls Bach: *Bach explains why he feels he should be allowed to leave the court of Duke Wilhelm August of Weimar.*

Prosecution: *Cross examines.*

Closing statements: *Each of the lawyers tries to convince the jury in a brief summary why Bach should or should not be released from jail.*

Judge gives final instructions to the Jury: *Judge should instruct jurors to base their decision on the evidence that has been given. The "burden of proof" rests upon the prosecutor—a man/woman is innocent until proven otherwise.*

The Jury begins the deliberation process. *Normally the jury would be sent to closed quarters, but since this is a mock trial, the jury will argue the case in front of the classroom. The selected jury foreman will make sure all the evidence is covered and be responsible for tallying the votes.*

Judge: *(After the jury has reached a decision.)* Are you ready to hand down a decision?

Jury Foreman: We are, Your Honor

Judge: How do you find the defendant?

Jury Foreman: *Instruct the foreman to deliver the verdict and tell how the jury reached it.*

* * * * * * * * *

Was the decision unanimous? _____

Do you believe Johann Sebastian Bach should remain the employee of Duke Wilhelm August of Weimar, or should he be allowed to become the employee of Prince Leopold von Anhalt-Köthen?

Why? _____

_____

_____

_____

_____

Student Name: _____

NATIONAL MUSIC STANDARD 9

Bumblebee Blast!

✶ **Introducing the Music of Rimsky-Korsakov for Both Upper and Lower Grade Levels**

Time Needed:
Approximately 45 minutes

Objective:
The students will be introduced to the music of Rimsky-Korsakov through the use of imagery and by listening to one of his popular compositions.

Resources Needed:
- Computer with Internet access and speakers (or, if available, a computer lab)
- *Flight of the Bumblebee* recording: classicsforkids.com/music/music_view.asp?id=25
- For lower grade level students, student sheets and crayons

Lesson
1. Ask the students to stand up.
2. Next make the following statements.
   - ♪ If you weren't born in the spring, please sit down. After the students sit down, explain that the composer you're going to be learning about today was born on March 18, 1844.
   - ♪ All students stand again.
   - ♪ If you don't have an older brother, please sit down. This composer had a brother who was 22 years older than he was.
   - ♪ All students stand again.
   - ♪ If you do not take piano lessons please sit down. This composer started taking piano lessons at age 6.
   - ♪ All students stand again.
   - ♪ If you don't enjoy fairy tales please sit down. Although this composer was well known for his operas, symphonies, orchestral works, and songs, he often centered his music on Russian fairy tales.
   - ♪ All students stand again.
   - ♪ If you don't know anyone who has served in the navy please sit down. This composer served both as an officer in the Imperial Russian Navy, then later as a civilian inspector of the naval bands.
   - ♪ All students stand again.
   - ♪ Sit down if you've never taught someone how to do something you're good at. This composer helped mentor several talented musicians, including Stravinsky.
   - ♪ All students may sit.
3. Ask students to raise their hand if they stood for more than one, two, three, or four statements. This will determine which student(s) have the most in common with Nikolai Andreyevich Rimsky-

Teaching Music Across History

Korsakov, a famous Russian composer during the Romantic period. One of his best-known compositions is called *Scheherazade,* a symphonic suite.

4. Instruct the students to listen to an orchestral interlude from an opera titled *The Tale of the Tsar Saltan.*

    ♪ For upper grade level students, have them write a short story describing what they think Rimsky-Korsakov might have been trying to portray in this composition. After the students have completed their stories, let them share their ideas.

    ♪ For lower grade level students, have them color either the turtle or the bee, based on their interpretation of the music.

5. Finally, share with the class that the name of the piece they just heard is "Flight of the Bumblebee." This music was portrays a scene in which the Tsar's son is turned into a bee by a magical swan so that he can fly to his father, as illustrated in the lyrics below.

>
Well, now, my bumblebee, go on a spree,
>
>Catch up with the ship on the sea,
>
>Go down secretly,
>
>Get deep into a crack.
>
>Good luck, Gvidon, fly,
>
>Only do not stay long!

6. Tell students Rimsky-Korsakov died on June 8, 1908.

Student Name: _____

Listen to the music. Do you think the composer was trying to portray the bee or the turtle? Color the picture you think is correct.

Teaching Music Across History | 93

Nursery Rhymes

NATIONAL MUSIC STANDARD 1 & 9

★ **Singing and Discovering the Components of a Nursery Rhyme Song**

Time Needed:
Approximately two class periods

Objective:
The students will develop an understanding of the origins of several nursery rhyme songs.

Resources Needed:
✂ Student sheets
✂ Colored paper (optional)
✂ Crayons
✂ Stapler

Lesson:
1. Explain the definition of a nursery rhyme song to the students.

    ♪ A nursery rhyme song is a children's rhyme that has been set to a simple melody.

2. Discuss and sing the following songs.

    ♪ "Old MacDonald Had a Farm" is a delightful nursery rhyme song that was first published in the U.S. in 1917. It is a cumulative song that layers specific portions at the end of each verse using the sounds of animals. Two other examples of cumulative songs include "The Twelve Days of Christmas" and "There Was an Old Lady Who Swallowed a Fly."

    ♪ "Lucy Locket" is a traditional English song. The rhyme was written in the mid-1800s and set to a simple melody. (At the time, a "pocket" was a small bag carried by a person—today it is referred to as a purse.)

    ♪ "Rain, Rain, Go Away" is thought to have originated in the United Kingdom as early as the 17th century. There are numerous versions of this rhyme, which is sung in many different countries today.

    ♪ "Mary Had a Little Lamb" is one of the most popular nursery rhyme songs in our country today. There appears to be some controversy over who actually wrote the poem. Some attribute the first four lines to John Roulstone—a student preparing for college who supposedly witnessed the hilarious event of Mary bringing a lamb to school—and credit the additional verses to Mrs. Sarah Josepha Hale. Another theory is that the entire poem was written by Mrs. Sarah Josepha Hale, who published the poem in May 24, 1830.

    ♪ "Twinkle Twinkle Little Star" is set to the melody of a French folk song that also caught the attention of Mozart, who composed 12 variations based on the tune titled "Ah vous dirai-je, Maman." This same melody is also used for "Baa Baa Black Sheep" and the "Alphabet Song."

3. Teach "Nursery Rhyme Medley" to the children and have sing it with you. They can use the coloring sheets to follow along with the lyrics.

4. Have them color the nursery rhyme song sheets. As an option, you can add two pieces of blank colored paper for a front and back, and then staple the sheets in between to form a book. The students may then decorate the front page with a picture of their favorite nursery rhyme song.

5. Sing the song medley again.

Old MacDonald Had a Farm

Old MacDonald had a farm,

Ee-eye, ee-eye oh!

And on that farm he had some chicks,

Ee-eye, ee-eye oh!

With a chick chick here, and a chick chick there,

Here a chick, there a chick, eve-ry-where a chick chick.

Old MacDonald had a farm, ee-eye, ee-eye oh!

Lucy Locket

Lucy Locket lost her pocket;

Kitty Fisher found it;

There was not a penny in it,

But a ribbon round it.

Mary Had A Little Lamb

Mary had a little lamb, little lamb, little lamb,

Mary had a little lamb its fleece was white as snow.

Teaching Music Across History

Twinkle, Twinkle, Little Star

Twinkle, twinkle, little star,

How I wonder what you are!

Up above the world so high,

Like a diamond in the sky.

Twinkle, twinkle, little star,

How I wonder what you are!

Nursery Rhyme Medley

Arranged by Valeaira Luppens

Ma-ry and Lu-cy were sis-ters two, They lived on a farm and they had lots to do! Old Mac-Don-ald was their Dad's first name, When-ev-er he called all the an-i-mals came! And they'd sing Old Mac-Don-ald had a farm,

Teaching Music Across History 99

ee-eye, -ee-eye oh! And on that farm he had some chicks, ee-eye-ee-eye-oh! With a chick chick here and a chick chick there, Here a chick, there a chick, eve-'ry where a chick chick, Old Mac-Don-ald had a farm, Ee-eye, ee-eye oh!

Ma-ry and Lu-cy were sis-ters two, They

100 Teaching Music Across History

lived on a farm and they had lots to do! One day Lu-cy was quite up-set, She started to wor-ry and she star-ted to fret! And they'd sing Lu-cy Lock-et lost her pock-et: Kit-ty Fish-er found it. There was not a pen-ny in it, But a rib-bon round it! Ma-ry and Lu-cy were sis-ters two, They lived on a farm and they had lots to do! The rain poured down and the sky turned grey, So both the sis-ters ran in-side to play! And they'd sing Rain, rain, go a-way, Come a-gain a-no-ther day! Ma-ry and Lu-cy were sis-ters two, They lived on a farm and they had lots to do!

102 Teaching Music Across History

One day when they ar-rived at school, Ma-ry's lamb came which broke all the class-room's rules!

And they'd sing Ma-ry had a lit-tle lamb, lit-tle lamb, lit-tle lamb,

Ma-ry had a lit-tle lamb its fleece was white as snow.

Ma-ry and Lu-cy were sis-ters two, They

Teaching Music Across History

104　Teaching Music Across History

NATIONAL MUSIC STANDARD 9

The Voice of the Pioneers

★ **A Brief Overview of the Popular Music Enjoyed by the Pioneers**

Time Needed:
Approximately 30 minutes

Objective:
Using a game format, the students will be introduced to the origins of songs enjoyed by the pioneers.

Resources Needed:
✂ Teacher sheet
   Optional: Recordings of folk songs listed in this lesson
   Optional: Incentive for winning team(s)

Lesson
1. Begin by explaining that music commonly expresses the struggles, conquests, and emotional feelings that we, as a society, experience. Ask the students to list some of their favorite songs that exemplify some of the feelings they are experiencing today. For example, I searched Google for songs written about 9/11 and found over 10 songs, including ones by Paul McCartney ("Freedom") and Bruce Springsteen ("Rising") written to commemorate the event. Popular songs expressing feelings include "Over the Rainbow," which is sung by Judy Garland and describes our dreams, or even "Bad Day," which is sung by Daniel Powter and portrays our more difficult moments.

2. Tell the students they will be playing a game based on the music of the pioneers.
   ♪ Divide the class in half and decide who will go first.
   ♪ The first team will receive up to five clues that will describe a popular pioneer song. The fewer clues they are given before they figure it out, the more points they will receive. For example, if the correct answer is given after the first clue, they will receive 50 points. After the second clue, they'd get 40 points; third clue, 30 points; etc.
   ♪ The team will work together as a group, but only one guess can be given after each clue. You may want to select a team captain for each group.
   ♪ If the song has not been solved after all the clues have been given, the second team gets a chance to steal the full 50 points by answering correctly.
   ♪ The second team will now get a chance to solve the clues for the next song.
   ♪ The teams alternate until the game is over.
   ♪ Tabulate the final score.

3. After the completion of this lesson, sing and/or dance to some of the folk songs listed in this unit.

The Voice of the Pioneers Clues

1. Home on the Range

Free Clue: The lyrics of this famous song were written by Higley Brewster and the music was composed by Daniel E. Kelly.

Clue 1: On May 20, 1862, President Lincoln signed the Homestead Act. This made it possible for any citizen, or anyone becoming a citizen, to purchase up to 160 acres of land for 10 dollars.

Clue 2: The land was in the plains area. There were no forests that would have provided lumber for their cabins. Buffalo roamed freely over the lands.

Clue 3: The lyrics of this song were first published in December 1873, and described a peaceful area where the deer and the antelope played freely.

Clue 4: The people in this song seldom complained. They hardly ever said a discouraging word.

Clue 5: Today this is the state song of Kansas and is often referred to as the unofficial song of the old American West.

2. Pop! Goes the Weasel

Free Clue: This song dates back as far as 1853, and is described as an old English dance tune. Over the years, the lyrics have been changed.

Clue 1: In Britain, this song was used as a singing game played in a similar fashion to musical chairs. The children danced around the room until they heard the last line. At that point they had to rush to jump into a ring. There was always one less ring than there were children.

Clue 2: During the 1850s, the song reached America, and the lyrics were changed. Both the old and the new versions refer to a monkey who likes to have fun.

Clue 3: The American lyrics also mention either a cobbler or a mulberry bush and a spool of thread.

Clue 4: The last line in every verse is the same. The one-syllable word sounds somewhat explosive followed by a reference to a weasel.

Clue 5: This melody is often used for jack-in-the-box toys.

3. Goodnight, Ladies

Free Clue: Edwin Pearce Christy has been given credit for writing this song in 1847.

Clue 1: This light-hearted song was written to be performed in a minstrel show, and was probably the last song of the evening.

Clue 2: The song originally had three verses which bid the ladies adieu.

Clue 3: In the second verse, the lyrics are altered as the gentlemen wish the ladies a fond farewell.

Clue 4: In the third verse, the gentlemen wish sweet dreams to the ladies. Today this verse is often replaced with "merrily we roll along."

Clue 5: This song was sung as a "partner song" with "Pick-a-Little" in the popular Broadway musical *The Music Man*.

4. I've Been Workin' on the Railroad

Free Clue: This American folk song was first introduced as a "levee song" and was published in 1894. A levee is a natural or man made embankment, next to a river, that prevents flooding.

Clue 1: This song talks about the job these men had, which helped lead to the western expansion.

Clue 2: These lyrics describe the long hours of labor the men were required "all the live long day."

Clue 3: The folk songs from this era were often written to make people feel better as they performed the demanding jobs they had. In this song the workers were primarily African-Americans and immigrants (often Irish) who were responsible for laying track down.

Clue 4: Another verse was later added to the end of this song, which may have been adapted from the melody of "Goodnight, Ladies." This verse describes a woman named Dinah who is in her kitchen.

Clue 5: This may well be the most famous train song written about the American railway.

5. Crawdad Song

Free Clue: This is a popular Southern children's folk song.

Clue 1: Life was often difficult for the early settlers. There wasn't much recreational time, but they did have "play-parties" from time to time. This particular song was written to accompany one of these events.

Clue 2: In this whimsical song, a boy and girl are getting a pole and a line to go fishing.

Clue 3: The title of this song centers on freshwater crustaceans that breathe through their gills.

Clue 4: These crustaceans live in fresh water streams and are quite delicious to eat.

Clue 5: One of the verses in this song describes a man who has an entire bag filled with these critters, but unfortunately he falls down, and the crustaceans crawl back into the water.

6. Yankee Doodle

Free Clue: This was a pre-revolutionary war song which may have been set to a melody from a nursery rhyme.

Clue 1: This song was said to be sung by the British when they marched against the colonists.

Clue 2: The British first sang this song to insult the rebels and the way they were dressed.

Clue 3: The rebels turned the tables on the British by adding lyrics to the song and making it their own.

Clue 4: The word "doodle," which is used in this song, is reported to be derived from a German word meaning "fool."

Clue 5: President Kennedy bought a pony for his daughter Caroline while living in the White House, and named the animal "Macaroni" after the pony in this song.

7. Skip to My Lou

Free Clue: This was an early American play-party dance.

Clue 1: In the communities where early American Protestants lived, dancing, especially to instrumental music using the fiddle, was simply not allowed—that instrument was often viewed as the devil's tool. The young people relied on "play-parties" to get around this. They sang while the audience clapped, creating their own music, and acted and danced to simple songs that were often tolerated. In this particular song, a gentleman stands in a ring pretending to look for a partner.

Clue 2: One of the verses refers to shooing flies away from dairy products.

Clue 3: In another verse, they discuss repainting their wagon from red to blue.

Clue 4: In one of the more familiar verses, the boy loses his partner, so he declares that he will find a prettier girl to replace her.

Clue 5: "Loo" is the Scottish word for love. Many feel that "Loo" was changed to "Lou" as American culture emerged and developed.

8. She'll Be Coming 'Round the Mountain

Free Clue: This song is thought to have originated from an old African American spiritual called "When the Chariot Comes" during the late 1800s.

Clue 1: After the song spread to the Appalachians, the lyrics were changed to reflect the beautiful surroundings of the mountainous area and the lifestyle of the people.

Clue 2: The form of this song is very similar to a call and response song. The first line is usually sung by a leader, and then the last three words in the line are repeated by a group of singers.

Clue 3: This song is relating a story about a guest who is about to arrive, what she'll look like, and the treatment she will receive once she gets there.

Clue 4: In more modern versions, sound effects have been added to replace the repeating of words (for instance, the repetition of "yum, yum" in response to eating chicken and dumplings).

Clue 5: It has been reported that the laborers who built the railroads in the Midwest sang this song in the late 1800s.

9. Fifteen Years on the Erie Canal

Free Clue: This song, written by Thomas S. Allen, was written to preserve the memory of this historical advancement.

Clue 1: One problem that was addressed in the early 1800s was how to improve the travel between New York City and the Great Lakes. The solution was to create a waterway, or canal, which is the focus of this song.

Clue 2: Canals are not natural waterways like rivers are; they are man made and constructed for the purpose of linking two bodies of water together.

Clue 3: The canal referred to in this song was constructed entirely by horses and humans, and it was a long and arduous process.

Clue 4: When this song refers to a "low bridge," it is actually warning people to get out of the way so they won't get hurt.

Clue 5: This song describes the life of a man and his mule named Sal who both spent 15 years on this canal.

NATIONAL MUSIC STANDARD 9

All That Jazz!

Time Needed:
Approximately 45 minutes

Objective:
Students will explore the roots of jazz.

Resources Needed:
- Computer with Internet access and speakers (or, if available, a computer lab)
- *Journeys into Jazz:* jazzinamerica.org/HerbieHancock
- *History of Jazz:* joy2learn.org/jazz/
- *Jazz at Lincoln Center's Nesuhi Ertegun Jazz Hall of Fame:* jalc.org/halloffame/
- Student sheet
- Pencils,
- Crayons
- colored pencils, and/or markers

Lesson
TECHNOLOGY: Watch Journeys into Jazz: **jazzinamerica.org/HerbieHancock**
1. As a whole group (or individually with computer lab), instruct the students to explore jazz in America by exploring the Journeys into Jazz Herbie Hancock link. This site takes the students on an animated time machine journey. The following is an overview of the virtual trip.
   - 1900 New Orleans
   - Plantations in the South
   - Emancipation Proclamation
   - Worship service
     A. Gospel
     B. Call and response
     C. Jazz is about feeling
   - Scott Joplin
     A. Left hand steady beat/ragged right hand
     B. Piano rolls (the first mechanically reproduced music)
     C. Ragtime
   - Congo Square
     A. Cake Walk
     B. New Orleans Jazz National History Park
     C. Louis Armstrong
     D. Sydney Bechet

Teaching Music Across History

- ♪ Jazz funeral band
- ♪ Early jazz
    - A. Louis Armstrong
    - B. Sydney Bechet
    - C. Collective improvisation
- ♪ Quiz
    - A. Jazz was born **about 100 years ago**.
    - B. Jazz was born in what city? **New Orleans**
    - C. Jazz's most important element is **improvisation**.
    - D. The music that led up to and eventually became jazz includes:
        - a) Work songs
        - b) Blues and gospel music
        - c) Ragtime
        - d) Brass marching band music
        - e) **All of the above**
    - E. The most important ragtime pianist and composer was **Scott Joplin**.
    - F. The first great jazz soloist was cornet/trumpet player **Louis Armstrong**.

2. *TECHNOLOGY:* Watch History of Jazz: **joy2learn.org/jazz/**
    - ♪ If you want to skip directly to History of Jazz, click "next" and you will be taken to the overview screen with the topics **Wynton, The Trumpet, History of Jazz, Nuts & Bolts of Jazz,** and **Jazz Musicians**.
    - ♪ The following is an overview of the "*History of Jazz.*"
        - A. Origins of jazz
            - African rhythms and European melodies
            - Marching bands
            - Funeral and church music
            - Minstrel groups
        - B. Ragtime
        - C. Bebop
        - D. Free jazz
        - E. Latin jazz
        - F. Fusion
        - G. Quiz 1
            - **New Orleans** is the birthplace of jazz.
            - This music is an example of **Latin** music.
            - The name *bebop* comes from **the vocalization of the instrumental line**.
            - This music is an example of **march** music.
            - Ragtime music is
                - a) From the Midwest

Teaching Music Across History

       b) Piano music

       c) The most American-sounding music

       d) **All of the above.**

♪ Wynton believes that funeral music can be **happy and sad**.

   H. Online Quiz 2

- An important aspect of African music is **ritual**.
- True or false: Wynton says spirituals are related to English fiddle songs. **False**
- True or false: Fusion was created in the 1960s when hip-hop emerged and was embraced by jazz musicians. **False**
- What does Wynton mean when he says, "The minstrel tradition today is now in rap music?" **Rap music patronizes blacks**.
- This music is an example of **ragtime** music.
- Many jazz fans consider bebop to be **the beginning of the modern era of jazz**.

3. *TECHNOLOGY*: Open the jukebox at **jalc.org/halloffame/**

♪ Students may listen to the great jazz artists while they complete the worksheet that follows.

♪ *Optional: As a model for students, display a clarinet, trumpet, African drum, and an example of a syncopated rhythm.*

♪ Display maps on a bulletin board or in the hallway during the month of April, which is *Jazz History Month*.

Student Name: _____

On the map of the United States, create a jazz logo including the elements and influences of jazz. The design can be anywhere on the map and should represent each of the following:

African drums	**Plantations (farm)**	**Marching Bands**
Trumpets	**Clarinets**	**The Cakewalk (dance)**

Jazz is a style of music that began in New Orleans, Louisiana, around 1900. It has developed to become more complicated in rhythm, texture (the thickness or thinness of sound), improvisation (spontaneous creation of music, within a structure), melody, and harmony.

Teaching Music Across History

NATIONAL MUSIC STANDARD 9

His Truth Is Marching On

Time Needed:
Approximately 30 minutes

Objective:
Students will read the biography of two historic women who were successful in a man's world, then try to draw conclusions for how women will achieve equal rights in third world countries.

Resources Needed:
- Computer with Internet access and speakers (or, if available, a computer lab)
- "Battle Hymn of the Republic" video: **archive.org/details/battle_hymn_of_the_republic**
- Student sheets
- Pencils

Lesson:
1. Watch the video "Battle Hymn of the Republic" and point out the following famous landmarks.
    - Tomb of the Unknown Soldier (Arlington Cemetery, Washington, D.C.)
    - Capitol Building (Washington, D.C.)
    - Lincoln Memorial (Washington, D.C.)
    - Statue of Liberty (New York City)
    - Mount Rushmore (near Keystone, South Dakota)
    - Kennedy Space Center (Florida)
    - Arlington Cemetery (Washington, D.C.)
    - Vietnam War Memorial (Washington, D.C.)
    - Marine Corps War Memorial (raising flag at Iwo Jima) (Washington, D.C.)
    - Washington Monument (Washington, D.C.)
    - Potomac River (Washington, D.C.)
    - Jefferson Monument (Washington, D.C.)

2. The lyrics (or words) to the song "The Battle Hymn of the Republic" were written by a woman named Julia Ward Howe, which was unusual for women of that time period.

3. Pass out the student sheets and read her biography.

4. There was also another woman who broke tradition and became a famous musician. Her name is Clara Schumann. Read her biography as well.

5. After reading the biographies, discuss which character traits these women had in common: dedication, bravery, strong work ethic, etc.

6. Finally, ask the students to write a brief answer to this essay question: How can women in third world countries achieve their freedom? Answers will vary: protest, assistance from developed nations, flee the country, etc.

7. Encourage students to restate the question and write their answer in complete sentences.

Teaching Music Across History

Julia Ward Howe

Julia Ward Howe was born in New York City, New York, on May 27, 1819. Her father was a wealthy banker.

Julia had a very cultured and strict upbringing. Her father cultivated her interest in education and expected her to do well in her studies. Julia was tutored at home and in private schools. As a child, Julia enjoyed writing, especially prose. At the age of 17, she began writing for magazines. She learned several different languages and made it a point to keep up on current events. Julia's father was aware of her brilliance and was very strict.

Julia continued to write after she married. At first she published some of her works anonymously because women were not encouraged to write during this time period, but she was quickly discovered because of her writing style, and from that time on she used her own name. She had six children.

Julia married a doctor named Samuel Gridley Howe who was a reformer. He believed that the wealthy should help the needy. Julia and her husband both supported Abraham Lincoln's stand against slavery during the Civil War. She was inspired to write the lyrics for "The Battle Hymn of the Republic" after watching a unit of Union troops marching in the Grand Review of the Armies. She used the melody of the song "John Brown's Body." Her song was first sung in 1862, for George Washington's birthday, and was printed in the *Atlantic Monthly* in February of that same year. She received $25 dollars for the submission.

When Julia died in 1910, the Massachusetts Thirtieth Infantry Band sang "The Battle Hymn of the Republic" at her funeral. They honored Julia because she had been an advocate for causes of human liberty for over half a century.

Clara Schumann

Clara Schumann was born in Leipzig, Germany, on September 13, 1819. Clara's father owned and operated a piano store. He began teaching her piano lessons at the age of five and by the time she was 8, she had to practice three hours a day. Even at this young age, her father recognized how musically gifted she was. She was only allowed to play with her two younger brothers.

Clara was tutored at home for her studies, and taken for walks daily. At the young age of 12, Clara started performing and touring in Europe. Her father became her manager and made arrangements for everything from hotels to stay in to concert hall performances. She received precious gifts for herself and her family. She loved the applause and the beautiful dresses she got to wear.

Clara fell in love with one of her father's piano students. Although she played better than Robert, he was better at composition. After writing love letters to each other over a long period of time, they were married. After marriage, Clara continued to perform and compose music, even though she had eight children. Robert also became more renowned for his music. Because of health issues, at one point Robert had to be hospitalized. Clara was devastated when her husband had to leave, but started performing again in order to support her family. Unfortunately, her husband died several years later.

Clara toured for 45 years after her husband's death. She enjoyed playing her husband's compositions at her concerts, which made his music even more popular. She had many close friendships with other musicians, such as Johannes Brahms.

Clara performed her last concert in 1896. Before her death, she suffered from several strokes. The last music she heard was her husband's. Music was her life and she excelled in it in a man's world.

Student Name: _____

Women's Rights

As you have read from the biographies of Julia Ward Howe and Clara Schumann, some women of the past were able to achieve success regardless of the traditional roles of women in their time period. Today, many countries do not recognize women's equal rights or equal treatment under the law. What do you think could be done to help women achieve their equal rights? Restate the question in your answer and use complete sentences.

_____

_____

_____

_____

_____

_____

_____

NATIONAL MUSIC STANDARD 9

The Treble Talk Show!

✶ **Researching the Lives of Famous Composers**

Time Needed:
Approximately 2 to 3 class periods

Objective:
Using a talk show format and working in pairs, the students will both research and present historical information on a well-known composer.

Resources Needed:
- Teacher demo sheet
- Student sheets
- As a suggested reference, *One-Page Composer Bios: 50 Reproducible Biographies of Famous Composers,* by Jay Althouse
- Pencils
- Two tall teacher stools
- *Optional:* microphone

Lesson:
1. Before the class begins, decide how the composers to be studied for this unit will be selected.
    - ♪ Do you want the students to select their own composer with your approval? (This allows the students to have a degree of ownership in the activity.)
    - ♪ Would you prefer to select the musicians yourself? (This avoids duplications and allows for focusing on a specific group of musicians or time period. If you decide on this option, write the composers' names down on small pieces of paper and allow the students to draw the names out of a drum.)
    - ♪ Provide each pair of students with a bio of their composer from *One-Page Composer Bios: 50 Reproducible Biographies of Famous Composers,* by Jay Althouse.

2. Explain to the students that they will be pairing up to put on a talk show in which a famous historical composer is interviewed. In each pair, one student will play talk show host and the other will play the composer.

3. After distributing the student worksheets and pencils, demonstrate to the class what they will be doing by playing the role of Brahms and choosing a student to play host as he/she interviews you. (See the teacher example that follows.)

4. Divide the students into pairs and provide them with the resources necessary to complete their research. Encourage them to be creative and to try to make the material they gather sound interesting. Allow them 30 minutes to complete this task.

5. Upon completing their research, allow the students additional time to practice delivering their lines out loud.

6. During subsequent class periods, the students will perform their interviews in front of the class.

- ♪ Allow the students presenting to sit on the stools.
- ♪ The students may use microphones if desired. This allows an opportunity for them to become more familiar with the equipment.

7. If time allows, play a few examples of several of the composers' music.
8. An option is to videotape the students and allow them to watch the interviews at a later date. Not only can this be used as an entertaining teaching tool, it will also help the students retain the information they heard by reinforcement.

The Treble Talk Show!
(Teacher Example)

Host: Good afternoon! My name is _____ and I would like to welcome you to another exciting episode of *The Treble Talk Show!* Today we are fortunate enough to have a famous composer with us. Would you like to tell the audience your name?

Composer: My name is Johannes Brahms.

Host: Please tell us when and where you were born.

Composer: I was born on May 7, 1833, in Hamburg, Germany.

Host: What instrument or instruments did you first learn to play and who was your first teacher?

Composer: My father was my first teacher. I was quite young when he discovered that I was a child prodigy and had a natural talent for the piano. I also studied under Otto Cossel and Edward Marxsen.

Host: How old were you when you wrote your first composition?

Composer: Hmm. I was 11 or 12 years old, but after I wrote them I destroyed them because I am quite a perfectionist.

Host: Tell the audience about your music.

Composer: I'd love to. My music was written during the Romantic period. I wrote a wide variety of music including chamber music, piano concertos, symphonies, and choral literature.

Host: When were you finally acclaimed as a success by your critics?

Composer: Probably at the premiere of "A German Requiem," a large choral work. It was well-received and, from that point on, I made quite a lot of money, even though I didn't spend much on myself. I preferred the simple life. I did like to support my friends and other music students though.

Host: Were you ever married? Do you have any children?

Composer: Unfortunately, although there were several women I admired, I remained a bachelor throughout my life.

Host: Tell me something most people don't know about you.

Composer: I love walking outside, and have a weakness for candy. My clothes are always clean, but I must admit that sometimes I don't keep up with the current styles.

Host: What are you most proud of?

Composer: That my music has withstood the test of time and is still listened to today.

Note: If you can't find the information in your research, ask the teacher if you can revise the host's question(s) to demonstrate your knowledge of the composer.

The Treble Talk Show!

Host: Good afternoon! My name is _____ and I would like to welcome you to another exciting episode of *The Treble Talk Show!* Today we are fortunate to have a famous composer with us. Would you like to tell the audience your name?

Composer: _____

Host: Please tell us when and where you were born.

Composer: _____

_____

Host: What instrument or instruments did you first learn to play and who was your first teacher?

Composer: _____

_____

_____

Host: How old were you when you wrote your first composition?

Composer: _____

_____

_____

Teaching Music Across History

Host: Tell the audience about your music.

Composer: _____

_____

_____

Host: When were you finally considered a success by your critics?

Composer: _____

_____

_____

Host: Were you ever married? Do you have any children?

Composer: _____

_____

_____

Host: Tell me something most people don't know about you.

Composer: _____

_____

_____

Host: What are you most proud of?

Composer: _____

_____

_____

NATIONAL MUSIC STANDARDS 8 & 9

Give My Regards to Broadway!

Time needed:
Approximately 30 minutes

Objective:
Students will explore the beginnings of Broadway theatre and explore current, kid-friendly Broadway shows.

Resources Needed:
- Computer with Internet access and speakers (or, if available, a computer lab)
- Student sheets
- **broadway.com/shows/tickets/?category=kid-friendly**
- Pencil

Lesson:
1. Pass out student sheet "Give My Regards to Broadway!"
2. Take turns reading the history aloud.
   - Popcorn reading: Read the first paragraph and stop abruptly, having the entire class say the next missing word. (This is an additional tool to keep students' attention on the text.)
   - Take turns reading each paragraph, allowing students to be the readers. (This will give weaker readers the chance to stop on difficult words, while the entire class fills in the blank.)
3. **TECHNOLOGY:** After reading "Give My Regards to Broadway!" go to **broadway.com/shows/tickets/?category=kid-friendly**
   - The link will show current, kid-friendly Broadway shows with links to story plots, video, photographs, and information about the show.
   - With your help, students will write down the titles of current shows, write a summary of the show, then rate it based on their personal desire to see it. (Answers will vary.)

Give My Regards to Broadway!

Broadway is a street located in New York City, well-known for live theatre, spanning a 12-block theater district. In the early 1800s, it was filled with European immigrants performing plays and operettas from Europe. If you were to visit one of these early shows, you would probably have seen over-the-top acting and the audience *booing* and *hissing* at the villains. Famous books from the time period were often turned into plays, too.

In 1866, a European ballet troupe came to New York to perform at the Academy of Music. Before they could perform, the theater burned down, leaving the troupe without a place to perform. They were stranded in New York City, so they asked a show producer at Niblo's Garden (another theater) if they could be included in an upcoming show, *The Black Crook.* The show was transformed into a musical extravaganza set in Germany in the 1600s, so the ballerinas played the parts of dancing gypsies. The show was a huge hit, earning over *a million dollars.*

Electric marquees were introduced to Broadway in 1891. Soon after, all the theaters began to add the marquees to advertise their shows. In the early 1900s, Longacre Square had the first moving electric sign. *The New York Times* moved their headquarters to a new building in 1904, so Longacre Square was renamed Times Square, and nicknamed "The Great White Way" due to the electric signs.

In the provided chart, write the names of current Broadway shows found on the kid-friendly section of Broadway.com. Write a brief summary of each story and give a rating based on your personal desire to see it—1 star equals "not interested" and 4 stars equal "must see." *This is your personal preference.*

Student Name: _____

Title of Show:	Story Summary:	Rate the show: 1 star = *not interested* 4 stars = **must see!**
1.		☆ ☆ ☆ ☆
2.		☆ ☆ ☆ ☆
3.		☆ ☆ ☆ ☆
4.		☆ ☆ ☆ ☆
5.		☆ ☆ ☆ ☆
6.		☆ ☆ ☆ ☆
7.		☆ ☆ ☆ ☆

Teaching Music Across History

NATIONAL MUSIC STANDARD 9

Time Machine

★ **Pre- or Post-Test for Music History Unit**

Time Needed:
Approximately 15 minutes

Objective:
Students will categorize composers within four time periods: Baroque, Classical, Romantic, or Modern.

Resources Needed:
- Student "Dear Navigator" sheets
- Clue sheet
- CD player
- CD listening examples
  1. Bizet: March - "Trumpet and Drum," "Impromptu" (*Jeux d'enfants*)
  2. Copland: *A Lincoln Portrait* (excerpt)
  3. Corelli: *Badinerie*
  4. Mendelssohn: "Scherzo" (*from A Midsummer Nights' Dream*)
  5. Mozart: *Minuet*
  6. Smetana: *The Moldau*
  7. Strauss: *Tritsch Tratsch Polka*
- Four Signs: **Baroque Period, Classical Period, Romantic Period,** and **Modern Period**
- Composers' thank you note

Lesson:
1. This activity can serve as a pre- and post-assessment for a music history unit.
2. Clear a pathway for your students to be able to successfully move around the classroom.
3. Post four signs: *Baroque Period, Classical Period, Romantic Period,* and *Modern Period.*
   - ♪ The signs may be hung on the wall or from the ceiling.
4. Pass out student "Dear Navigator" sheets and read the directions as a group.
   - ♪ *Scenario*: Students will listen to four clues. When they think they can identify the right time period, they will *silently* drive their invisible time machines to the correct sign. If they arrive at the proper time period by the fourth clue, they will be able to rescue the composer, who is trapped in a time warp.
   - ♪ This will allow you to visually assess the students' understanding of the time period and frame the time periods with historical events for the students. Points for each correct answer can be given, but are not necessary.

Teaching Music Across History

5. Clues:
   - ♪ First, play an example of the composers' music to provide an aural clue for students.
   - ♪ After a few seconds, read clues to the students (or assign one or two student readers).
   - ♪ Give plenty of time for students to ponder their choice between clues, and also remember repeat clues. This allows students to change their minds/correct their response as more clues are read.
6. After the final clue, reveal the correct answer by driving *your* invisible time machine to the correct time period sign.
   - ♪ This task can be done by a student reader.
   - ♪ To make it more entertaining as the clue-giver drives the invisible time machine to the right answer, he or she can move around from period to period and finally hold up the thank you note from the composer.
   - ♪ Students should return to the center of the room for the process to continue.
   - ♪ Restate the name of the composer and their musical time period before continuing to the next composer.

Dear Navigator,

HELP! The International Society of Time Travelers (ISTT), developer of the Invisible Time Machine, needs your help to steer to the correct time periods to save eight composers from a time warp! You'll be given four clues to find the correct time period for each of the eight rescue attempts.

1. The first and most important clue will be *the composer's music*. **Baroque music** (1600–1750), usually has a fancy melody line. **Classical music** (1750–1825) has a lighter texture than baroque music and is simpler in style. Classical music has a larger orchestra than the baroque period, as well. **Romantic music** (1825–1900) saw continued growth in the orchestra along with freer musical expression and songlike melodies. Finally, **Modern music** (1900–present) doesn't really have a common style. It includes the beginning of jazz and rock 'n' roll music.
2. The second clue will be the composer's names and the country he or she is from.
3. The third clue will be an important historical event from that time period.
4. The final clue will be the composer's *date of death*. (The composer will probably have died before the ending date of their time period.)

Try to find the correct time period BEFORE the composer's death date is announced! You may change your mind as more information is revealed, but we're counting on you to safely navigate your invisible time machine to the correct time period and save the composers!

Thank you!

The International Society of Time Travelers

Clue 1 The MUSIC	Clue 2 Name & Country of Origin	Clue 3 Historical Event During That Time Period	Clue 4 Date of Death (answer)
March – (Bizet)	George Bizet, France	American Civil War	1875 (Romantic)
Lincoln Portrait, excerpt (Copland)	Aaron Copland, USA	World War I and II	1990 (Modern)
Badinerie (Corelli)	Arcangelo Corelli, Italy	King Charles II of England grants a charter for the Carolina colonies	1713 (Baroque)
Scherzo (Mendelssohn)	Felix Mendelssohn, Germany	The Underground Railroad was established in America	1847 (Romantic)
Minuet (Mozart)	Wolfgang Amadeus Mozart	The Declaration of Independence was signed	1791 (Classical)
The Moldau (Smetana)	Bedřich Smetana, Czech Republic	American Civil War	1884 (Romantic)
Tritsch-Tratsch Polka (Strauss)	Johann Strauss, Jr., Austria	Abraham Lincoln was assassinated	1899 (Romantic)

Teaching Music Across History

Baroque Period (1600–1750)

Classical Period (1750–1825)

Romantic Period (1825–1900)

Modern Period (1900–present)

A big THANK YOU

134 Teaching Music Across History

CD Contents

1. *Badinerie* (Corelli)
2. *Minuet* (Mozart)
3. March – "Trumpet and Drum Impromptu," *Jeux d'enfants* (Bizet)
4. *The Moldau* (Smetana)
5. *Scherzo* (Mendelssohn)
6. *Tritsch-Tratsch Polka* (Strauss)
7. "In the Hall of the Mountain King," *Peer Gynt Suite* (Grieg)
8. "Ase's Death," *Peer Gynt Suite* (Grieg)
9. "Morning," *Peer Gynt Suite* (Grieg)
10. "Anitra's Dance," *Peer Gynt Suite* (Grieg)
11. "Overture," *Hansel and Gretel* (Humperdink)
12. "Arabian Dance," *Nutcracker Suite* (Tchaikovsky)
13. "Chinese Dance," *Nutcracker Suite* (Tchaikovsky)
14. "Dance of the Flutes," *Nutcracker Suite* (Tchaikovsky)
15. "Dance of the Sugar Plum Fairy," *Nutcracker Suite* (Tchaikovsky)
16. "March," *Nutcracker Suite* (Tchaikovsky)
17. "Overture," *Nutcracker Suite* (Tchaikovsky)
18. "Trepak," *Nutcracker Suite* (Tchaikovsky)
19. "Waltz of the Flowers," *Nutcracker Suite* (Tchaikovsky)
20. *Lincoln Portrait*, excerpt (Copland)

Lessons and CD Correlations

1. String Story
    a. *Badinerie* (Corelli)
2. Forward March
    a. March – "Trumpet and Drum Impromptu," *Jeux d'enfants* (Bizet)
3. Crack the Code
    a. *Badinerie* (Corelli)
    b. *Minuet* (Mozart)
    c. "In the Hall of the Mountain King," *Peer Gynt Suite* (Grieg)
    d. *Lincoln Portrait*, excerpt (Copland)
4. Peer Gynt Isn't Very Sweet!
    a. "In the Hall of the Mountain King," *Peer Gynt Suite* (Grieg)
    b. "Ase's Death," *Peer Gynt Suite* (Grieg)
    c. "Morning", *Peer Gynt Suite* (Grieg)
    d. "Anitra's Dance", *Peer Gynt Suite* (Grieg)
5. Hansel and Gretel
    a. "Overture," *Hansel and Gretel* (Humperdink)
6. Nutcracker Suite
    a. "Arabian Dance," *Nutcracker Suite* (Tchaikovsky)
    b. "Chinese Dance," *Nutcracker Suite* (Tchaikovsky)
    c. "Dance of the Flutes," *Nutcracker Suite* (Tchaikovsky)
    d. "Dance of the Sugar Plum Fairy," *Nutcracker Suite* (Tchaikovsky)
    e. "March," *Nutcracker Suite* (Tchaikovsky)
    f. "Overture," *Nutcracker Suite* (Tchaikovsky)
    g. "Trepak," *Nutcracker Suite* (Tchaikovsky)
    h. "Waltz of the Flowers," *Nutcracker Suite* (Tchaikovsky)
7. Chit Chat
    a. *Tritsch-Tratsch Polka* (Strauss)
8. Time Traveler
    a. March – "Trumpet and Drum Impromptu," *Jeux d'enfants* (Bizet)
    b. *Lincoln Portrait*, excerpt (Copland)
    c. *Badinerie* (Corelli)
    d. *Scherzo* (Mendelssohn)
    e. *Minuet* (Mozart)
    f. *The Moldau* (Smetana)
    g. *Tritsch-Tratsch Polka* (Strauss)

Music History Internet Resources

The following websites can be used by the teacher and/or students to explore music history and create long-lasting memories. Save them in your favorites or create hyperlinks on a webpage or blog for quick access.

- ♪ apassion4jazz.net Jazz history and education, including a timeline, definitions, podcasts, videos, a photo gallery, and an extensive festival/event guide.
- ♪ blabberize.com A site that will make historical information more interesting to students as they get it straight from a composer's mouth.
- ♪ classicsforkids.com/shows/past.asp Music history podcasts for student audiences featuring specific composers ranging from J.S. Bach to Ralph Vaughan Williams. Each podcast explores specific works or styles of music, providing short audio examples for students' understanding.
- ♪ classicalkusc.org/kids/brahms/base.htm An interactive site to teach kids about chamber music and Johannes Brahms in 1890s Vienna
- ♪ datadragon.com/day This Day in Music History feature that includes composer and musician birthdays, notable Broadway shows and plays, a references to significant chart toppings in popular music. Also useful is the "Pick Your Own Day" function at the bottom of the page.
- ♪ hypermusic.ca/ An exploration of classical music history from the Middle Ages to the 20th century, including the main periods, subtopics, forms, and composers important to classical music. Jazz history is also explored.
- ♪ keepingscore.org/interactive This web component to the Keeping Score television series connects classical music to the core curriculum. Tabs to explore include Composers, Musical Technique, History, and Musical Scores.
- ♪ last.fm/listen Free online radio that allows users to find recordings by searching the name of an artist, composer, or genre.
- ♪ learningobjects.wesleyan.edu/vim/ Explore the world musical instrument collection in the music department at Wesleyan University.
- ♪ library.thinkquest.org/15413/history/music-history.htm Covers music history by historical time periods and vocal, instrumental, and composer categories. The 20th century section is divided into trends, techniques, and composers
- ♪ library.thinkquest.org/22673/index.html This site highlights composers' finest symphonies. You can also listen to instruments of the orchestra and view a timeline with composer info.
- ♪ loc.gov/jukebox Historical recordings from the Library of Congress.
- ♪ music-with-ease.com Features biographical information on composers, composer images, multiple genres, games, and activities.
- ♪ nyphilkids.org/gallery/main.phtml An extensive composers gallery from the New York Philharmonic that is sortable by country, birthday, style, and name. Each entry includes an audio clip example of the composer's work.
- ♪ pbskids.org/chuck/ Chuck Vanderchuck's "Something Something" Explosion provides the history of musical genres (jazz, rock, salsa, country, etc.), timbre and rhythmic identification games, coloring pages, melodic dictation, and more.
- ♪ sbgmusic.com/html/teacher/reference/histor.html Silver Burdett Making Music provides a handy reference for 20th century American folk and rock music.
- ♪ timesearch.info Time Search is a searchable history resource that allows the user to search other websites by year, area, or theme (specifically for our purposes, Performing Arts: Music).
- ♪ wordle.net/create Wordle is a site for generating "word clouds" from text that you provide. This could be very useful for student music history reports or visuals to include in a lesson.

About the Authors

Valeaira Luppens served as an elementary music specialist in the Lee's Summit School District in Missouri for 20 years. She has been a recipient of the Expect the Best award, a district-wide honor for exemplary teaching and service. The award encompasses all disciplines and is awarded monthly to one outstanding staff member. Valearia earned her Bachelor of Music Education from Central Missouri State University and her Master of Educational Psychology in Research with an emphasis in gifted/talented studies from Kansas University. She has belonged to the National Association for Music Education (NAfME) throughout her teaching experience and received her certification from the American Orff-Schulwerk Association.

Gregory Foreman holds a Certificate of Piano Performance, a Bachelor of Music Education, and a Master of Arts in Teaching; and has completed 45 post-graduate hours in instructional technology integration and differentiated instruction. He is a member of NAfME and has been an elementary music specialist since 1984. He has also served as the Lead Teacher for the Lee's Summit Elementary Music Department, "Music in Education" Keyboard Lab Facilitator, Mentor Teacher, Professional Staff Development Affiliate, Technology Team Chairman, Building Web Manager, Adjudicator, and director of various children's choirs.

Mr. Foreman is the recipient of the Excellence in Teaching, Hertzog Leadership, and Learning for Life awards; has performed as soloist with the Kansas City Symphony, the UMKC Conservatory Orchestra, the Youth Symphony of Kansas City, National Public Radio, Kansas Public Radio, and the Kansas City Music Hall; and accompanies silent films annually at the Kansas Silent Film Festival at Washburn University in Topeka, Kansas.

Teaching Music Across History

Notes

Notes